M

Sarah's Secret:

A WESTERN TALE

OF BETRAYAL AND

FORGIVENESS

BEVERLY SCOTT

SWSM Press, San Francisco, CA

Published in the United States
Amazon edition published by Word Project Press
All other editions published by SWSM Press

Requests for permission to make copies of any part of this work should be submitted online at
bev@bevscott.com

Credits:
Cover Design: Deborah Purdue, Illumationdesigns.com
Cover Art: Tara Thelen
Interior Design: Melody W. Baker, Graphic Design by Melody
Author Photograph: Desmond Gribben

ISBN - 978-0-9833740-1-5

Also by Beverly Scott:
"Consulting on the Inside: A Practical Guide for Internal Consultants" Second Edition, co-authored with B. Kim Barnes, 2011
"Consulting on the Inside: An Internal Consultant's Guide to Living and Working Inside Organizations," 2000
"Quality Circles: How to Create Them. How to Manage Them. How to Profit from Them." Co-authored with Ron Kregoski, 1982

"Follow on"
www.facebook.com/bevscottwriter
www.linkedin.com/in/bevscott
www.pinterest.com/bevscottsf/
www.bevscott.com/blog/

DEDICATION

This book, *Sarah's Secret: A Western Tale of Betrayal and Forgiveness* is dedicated to my paternal grandmother, Eva Ellen Russell Scott, an inspiration and role model to me. Although she suffered from rheumatoid arthritis which crippled her painfully, she never complained. She wrote letters to me to encourage and congratulate me for my school grades; she listened and paid attention to my stories when I visited in person.

She struggled to raise her five children as a widow when women had few options for support. But she went back to the classroom which she had left when she married. She ultimately became the school superintendent in Thomas County, Nebraska. She may have been the first woman to hold such a position in Nebraska. She was courageous, strong, dedicated and humble.

This book is also dedicated to my daughter, Darby, her sons, Clayton and Jeremy and their descendants that they may have a compelling story about their ancestors.

ACKNOWLEDGEMENTS

An author writes alone but she needs a "Village" to finish a book. This book would have never been completed without the inspiration, support, encouragement and enthusiasm of others. I want to recognize some of those friends and supporters who helped me bring this project to fruition.

• The most important person in my life, my spouse and life partner, Courtney, who not only cheered me on as the days, months and years dragged on, but who served as my guide in the initial search for the mysteries of my family history as well as my companion in driving throughout the Midwest to find information and identify the sites where my grandparents lived.

• My daughter, Darby, who encouraged me and used Facebook to reach her friends with requests and information about my book.

• My late son-in-law, Aaron, who was so enthusiastic in reading the early chapters that he pulled out a $20.00 bill as a first installment on his investment in the success of the book.

• My grandsons, Clayton and Jeremy, who have listened to readings and given enthusiastic input on the title.

• My writing group, especially Kim and Jan, who read early chapters and versions, giving me feedback and helping me solve some of the puzzles of the plot.

- My editor, Elaine Beale, who gave me the feedback that I needed, telling me what worked well and what I needed to revise, drop or totally re-write.
- My beta-readers who read an early draft of the manuscript and gave me very helpful feedback.
- Robasciotti and Philipson who lease me an office in which to do my writing.
- My women's group "Systers", who listened and supported my slow plodding progress over the years.
- The expertise of Joe Vanderkooy, Judy Baker, Judy Reyes, Word Project Press and others who provided advice, support, administration and guidance in areas that are not my strong suit.
- Many family, friends and colleagues who subscribe to my blog, friend me on Facebook, or follow me on Linked-In who have helped promote the book, provided encouragement and contributed ideas for the title.

CONTENTS

FOREWORD

What My Grandmother Told Me

My grandmother told me that my grandfather, my father's father, died at the age of 70 when my dad was two. She evaded any other questions and I grew up knowing nothing about my grandfather. Years later, I discovered that he actually died when my dad was four, and that there was much more to the story than my grandmother was willing to disclose.

The pieces of the puzzle have gradually come together as family members, mostly my cousins, shared what they had heard. Also, an aunt who married into the family who was interested in genealogy discovered a previously unknown marriage and I found a treasure trove of documents in the National Archives in Washington, D.C.

Few members of my generation, born as the United States entered and fought World War II, have a grandfather who was born in 1840 and was a Civil War Veteran. My curiosity about this man, who was a shadowy figure to my father and his siblings, led to my efforts to trace my ancestry and pursue the genealogy of the family. This pursuit, along with elements of the story revealed in the many documents in the National Archives, and my frequent imaginary excursions into my grandfather's past to understand his actions, has resulted in my decision to write this book.

The story is like finding a skeleton in a musty old trunk. The bones are real but the flesh is long gone and the circumstances of how it happened to be put in the trunk are mysteriously unknown. Thus, the bones of this story are true but the flushing out of the context, human emotions and the reasons for decisions and impulses are created from my imagination. These are my efforts to put myself in the time period and the lives of the primary characters. These are the creations from my imaginary excursions, quiet moments of intuition, dreams and flights of inspiration, efforts to weave a credible yet engaging story about my grandparents.

PART 1: SARAH

Tucumcari, Quay County, New Mexico

January 20, 1911

ONE

The Day Sam Died

No, don't leave." Sam clawed at his blankets and croaked, "Stay with me. I need you here."

I frowned. "I need to see if Patricia is awake."

The last few weeks had been difficult. Sam had needed, no, demanded, that I stay beside him. I was weary of the struggle to care for him and still find time to meet the needs of all the children. He became agitated and irritated when he wanted something when I was busy with the baby or giving ten-year-old Charlie a reassuring hug.

I patted his hand and tucked the blankets around him. "Sam, I'll be right back. I need to see if Patricia is awake."

He clung to me so I sat back down to wait for him to doze off, listening for Patricia's whimpers.

Last night when I tried to sleep in the chair, Sam's moans and cries startled me awake. When I thought how little time I had left with him, my whole body shook and my heart went cold. He was burning up, so I folded down the covers and mopped his brow with cool water. Later he was chilled and shivering, grabbing at the covers to try to get warm again.

Today, the sun had brought some warmth to the crisp cool air. I needed to breathe and Sam's blankets needed to be aired out and the soiled bedding washed. He had dozed off again. Patricia was still napping.

Daniel hollered, "Water's hot, Ma!" As I came outside with the bedding, I paused to smell the coolness before walking toward the tub, which sat in the middle of the yard on a large brown rock. That rock had been flattened and smoothed by the wind and rain of a thousand winters. Daniel, at sixteen the oldest of my children, was pouring hot water into the tub.

He smiled down at me. He'd shot up so in the last year and now stands so tall, I have to throw my head back to look up at him. I smiled at his lanky frame. How awkward he seemed suddenly, trying to get comfortable in his tall body and big feet.

I put my hands into the water. "Ah, feels good." I began to wash the bedding and some of the boys' shirts.

"Daniel, will you and Joe wring these out and hang them up? They'll dry quickly with the sun out. This air sucks the moisture from everything."

He nodded, grabbing the clothes to wring them out. He was my willing helper, taking over the chores that I could no longer do. I wondered if he was beginning to be resentful. He had his father's quiet way and keen eye, noticing the slight expressions that flash in someone's eyes or the movement of the brush that hid the jack rabbit he might bring home for dinner.

Daniel kept a lot to himself. I knew I would need to

probe to find out how he was feeling, but I was too preoccupied to talk to him now. As I walked across the yard to return to Sam's bedside, I thought about how thankful I was for Daniel's calm and easy way with the little ones. He adored the baby. She quieted right down when he gathered her in his long arms to coo and tickle her. He guided and protected Petey, who is was weak and small for a four-year-old after a long bout with rheumatic fever. But he was not so good with Joe and Charlie.

"Joe, come and help with the laundry," Daniel yelled.

"Doin' somethin' else," Joe hollered back.

"Dammit Joe, why are ya so difficult? Both of us need to help Ma. Not just me."

"All right, I'm comin. But don't yell at me." Joe still resented Daniel ordering him around just like he did when he was four.

I paused at the door, hesitant to leave the fresh cool air. My eyes needed to adjust to the darkness. Although the lantern shed some light, I had to be careful. I put each foot on the narrow steps carved from the hard soil. I tended to lose my balance easily as I made my way into our underground home, and there was nothing for me to grab if I tripped.

Before going into the cave-like room in the back where Sam slept, I heard the whimpers and rustling of Patricia, waking up from her nap. Anxious to avoid disturbing Sam, I picked her up before she could cry.

"You're such an easy baby," I murmured to Patricia. "I'm so happy to have a girl after four boys." She smiled up at me as if she was in on my secret. "You are such a pretty girl." My love welled up and a tear dropped on her pale delicate face. Her dark eyes blinked with puzzlement. "I'm just lovin' you," I reassured her. As she nuzzled to find my left breast, I wondered how long my milk would last.

As I entered his room, filled with the stale smells of sweat, urine and sickness, Sam began mumbling again, then he cried out, "I won't answer! I won't answer. I am married ...." His voice trailed off to a mumble again and I caught what sounded like my name, "Sarah Armstrong Martin."

"What's that about?" I wondered aloud.

I hobbled quickly toward the bed, a thin mattress we brought with us from Oklahoma, worried that it was close to the end. I pulled a quilt around Sam's shoulders, held his hand and soothed his brow while I continued to nurse Patricia. He lay still now. Only his hands twitched occasionally. I studied him, listening to his labored breathing. His body was small and frail under the blanket. His skin drooped from his jaw. His eyes have sunk into his face, which was lined with the ravages of constant pain. They fluttered open, looking at me in recognition for a moment. Then they closed, and, with a release of breath, he was gone.

I sat quietly nursing Patricia, unable to move. My mind was empty. My heart ached. He was gone.

Finally, I got up to tell the children. After some tears, hugs and reassurance, I sent them all with Daniel into town for some supplies. I needed some time alone.

TWO

Afterwards

*I*n the afternoon, I gently washed Sam's thin body. His ribs had pushed against his skin. His knees looked like knobs on sticks. He had wasted away in the last weeks. I held his hand and stroked his withered finger, injured during the War. My tears and sadness flowed all over him as I washed him and whispered goodbye. I told him that despite his rough edges, he was good to me. I would miss his wisdom, his care and support, his companionship. Then I dressed him in his best pants and shirt. His black hair was only flecked with gray even now. I stared for a long time remembering the dark handsome man I married almost twenty years before.

Afterward, I stepped outside. The winter light was fading. From the door, I could just barely see the rocky brown hills. They seemed rude, pushing up through the dry grasslands, demanding that I notice them. No sign of human disturbance in this barren landscape except for our animal shed.

I felt myself shiver. The wind was unusually still for New Mexico, but the air was crisp and cold. I went back inside. I wanted to feel the heat from the fire in the stove. I wanted to be warm, really warm. I sat down in my rocking chair rocking slowly. The coldness inside moved up my back and tingled at the nape of my neck. I fingered the piece of Wyoming Jade Sam had given me when he proposed, remembering that he promised steadfast love.

"I'm a widow," I said aloud. I was alone, completely responsible for the children, not just for a few weeks or the winter season until Sam returned. I felt cold, flat. I opened my Bible, hoping for solace. I began to survey the landscape of my mind, much as I had the landscape outside. My mind was a closed book with all the memories of my life with Sam shut away. "I am alone." There were no images of the future. But to my surprise, I also felt a sense of calm and relief.

I stopped rocking. Was my relief because Sam was no longer suffering, or because I no longer felt torn between his demands and the children? I had known that he would leave me a widow given the thirty-year age difference between us.

I thought I had prepared myself to face many years without a husband. Now, I was annoyed that he had left me with five children, including an infant, with no means of support. Could I cope without him?

I straightened up remembering how I had steeled myself against my fear of being alone when we lived in Oklahoma. I had learned to cope with his long absences to meet with the government agent about his Veteran's pension. I reminded myself, that I had also loved my independence when I was young. Now, as I thought back to those times alone in Oklahoma facing the challenges of sick children, wandering livestock or bitter winter storms, I felt a calm and growing confidence that I could handle this challenge.

I rocked quietly now, continuing to feel the mixture of relief, sadness, resentment and fear. I felt the smoothness of the Jade in my apron pocket again. It had rough edges which Sam had compared to himself.

Soon the children would be home from town and Patricia would wake from her afternoon nap. The familiar knot in my back tightened. Being a woman alone with five children would be hard. It would be even harder to make ends meet. Would we even have enough to eat? Could I keep Daniel, Joe and Charlie from going off on their own and maybe getting into trouble? But I couldn't let myself get discouraged. They were good boys.

I reassured myself that I could handle this. I had to. I sat up straight. Together, as a family, we would be strong.

THREE

The Funeral

I had awakened with that knot in my back again and my stomach was churning. As I dressed, brushed my hair and wound it up on my head, a shiver moved through me. I wasn't sure if it was the cold or the emptiness that lay ahead.

I had coaxed the fire awake, blowing on it and throwing on some cow chips. Now, it burned with enthusiasm, warming up the room. All three boys reached out stiff fingers toward the heat while the body of their father lay covered by a quilt next to the wall. As I took a fresh batch of biscuits out of the oven, Daniel grabbed one and popped the whole thing in his mouth. The other boys copied their older brother.

"Where are your manners?" I demanded. Then I reminded myself they had just lost their father and I gave them a forgiving smile.

We sat around the table sharing fresh, warm milk and dunking biscuits. Patricia was sitting on my lap sucking on her fingers. When they'd finished eating, Petey asked, "Where did Papa go if he's dead?" It was a question I'd been dreading.

"He didn't go anywhere," Daniel said, jumping in before I could respond. "His body died. He can't go anywhere."

"But," Charlie said, his forehead was wrinkled in puzzlement, "what's it mean to go to Heaven? Maybe he's in Heaven."

"What's 'aven?" Petey asked.

I set my cup of tea on the table. "God, who created everything, including us, gives us a period of time on earth," I said. "When our time's up, our bodies die because our hearts stop beating. That's what happened to Papa. His heart stopped beating."

I needed to pause to hold myself together. I resented that I even had to have this conversation. I'd always relied on Sam's wisdom for questions like these. But now he was gone. I glanced at Sam's body then I looked at the boys. Daniel gazed at me with anticipation. Joe looked bored and stared off into empty space. Charlie's eyes were wide with curiosity while Petey was looking at me patiently, still waiting to learn about heaven.

I took a gulp of my tea and then plunged on. "The spirit that lives inside our bodies doesn't die like our bodies. It goes to live with God."

"So that's what Heaven is... living with God?" Charlie looked relieved.

"Yeah," Joe said, grinning as he looked over at Papa's body. "Up in the sky...that's where Pa is."

Daniel frowned. "Don't be funny, Joe,"

"I want my Papa," Petey wailed.

"Petey, come here," I said, handing Patricia to

Daniel and then gathering up Petey on my lap, rocking back and forth, soothing him, lightly rubbing his back.

"We all miss Papa," I said as I looked at my boys. Tears were silently rolling down Joe's and Charlie's faces. Daniel's face scrunched up and the tears soon welled up in his eyes and spilled onto his cheeks too. I opened my arms to gather them all in, swallowing hard. Then I let my own tears flow.

"But Ma, how're we going to make it?" Daniel cried. "We can't grow anything on this land!"

Petey's sobs had turned to hiccups now and the other boys were sniffling.

I needed to be strong. I sat up straight, breathed deeply and looked at each of my children. "I don't know for sure, but I do know this—we will be together and we will all be strong for each other." I paused and took a breath. "Now, let's get cleaned up and get dressed to go into town for the funeral."

I moved slowly to prepare to leave. My arthritis had gotten worse since Sam got sick and it was taking longer for my joints to loosen this morning. I felt very stiff.

"Joe, come and help me carry Pa out to the wagon," Daniel said.

Joe nodded his head and they prepared to carry their father to the wagon wrapped in one of my quilts.

"I want to help." Charlie went over to Sam's feet and grasped them. They lifted him gingerly at first. They seemed to assume he would be heavy—after all he had been a big man. But his illness had whittled him down to nothing. They were able to lift him easily.

After a brief service, Preacher Van led the small gathering in the Lord's Prayer. With the final "Amen," I prepared myself to receive the condolences from the few families who had come. They were all kind and well-meaning people. I wondered how it would feel to stay here among them in New Mexico.

Many of them asked me about my plans and I found myself repeating, "I haven't decided yet." Then Mrs. Argon came over and said to me in a loud whisper, "My dear, you shouldn't stay here. All the wives will worry every time you speak to their men. No one will trust you as a widow woman."

I winced and turned away.

Preacher Van overheard her cutting remark and hurried over. "Mrs. Martin, you know you are welcome to stay. Not everyone feels that way." He paused. "Still, you might be better off with your family in Nebraska."

I pulled my shawl around me and tried to swallow the ache in my throat as I stepped cautiously toward the wagon. The boys were waiting, shifting from one foot to another, shivering from the cold.

"I hate this place," Daniel said, pounding his fist on the wagon.

"Me too," Joe added as he walked away from his brothers.

"But where can we go?" Charlie whined.

"Oh, be quiet!" Daniel hissed.

I knew they didn't like it here, but did I really want to take my family on the long perilous journey back to Nebraska?

FOUR

❧

Preparing to Leave

April 1911

I waited several weeks before I made my decision. It was early spring, more than three months after Sam's funeral. The sun was warm–almost hot, and the days were longer. I realized that even if Sam was buried here, I wasn't part of this community. It was too lonely, not a place to raise my children. I hated that Sam had brought us here. The weather was miserable, nothing grew in this sandy, starving soil. Even the sagebrush struggled to find moisture. And we'd had to kill so many rattlesnakes.

The last time, I'd turned to find a snake coiled within inches of where the baby lay on a mat on the dugout floor. Sam was in Phoenix, the boys were in school and Petey was playing outside on the rocks. I grabbed a shovel and slammed it as hard as I could on the snake's head. Then I grabbed the baby and ran outside.

I'd never get used to it here and it would never feel like home. We would go back to Nebraska. I knew many people there. "Mama and I share your sadness in losing Sam. We hope you will consider coming home to Nebraska…" Papa had written to me in his last letter. I had a brother and a sister there, and I knew they'd be pleased to have us close by.

When my neighbors heard we were leaving, they had generously brought over dried meat, starter for bread, vegetables from their root cellars and a sack of flour. I was so grateful. The supplies would help us stretch our meager resources.

I was proud of the strong stand I took negotiating with Mr. McNab for a fair price for our two milk cows. He'd initially offered me a price so low it was insulting. But I just kept repeating the price I wanted, saying I thought it was fair. He finally came around. Since we needed the horses to pull our wagons, we didn't have much else to bring in money. Too bad I couldn't sell the homestead, but we hadn't lived on it long enough to "prove it up," to get the deed like we did in Nebraska and Oklahoma. We'd abandon it like so many others had done.

The thought of the unknown stretching out ahead of me made my back knot up. Crippled with arthritis and traveling alone with five children, I felt very vulnerable. I was terrified that we would run out of money and I was even more terrified that I'd lose one of the children. I sighed, straightened up, and repeated my frequent prayer, "Please God, give me the strength and courage to take my family back to Nebraska."

Nebraska, with the fields of corn growing tall, the prairie grass blowing in the wind and the sod houses that kept families warm in the winter and cool in the summer, that was my home. I could see the smile on Papa's face as he read my letter saying that we were coming back. He would grin from ear to ear, turn to Mama, read her the letter, and then exclaim, "Mama, they are coming home!" Mama's smile would light up her face. I imagined the beautiful contrast of that smile against her plain appearance with her dark clothes and severe hair style. As Quakers, we didn't believe in adornment but Mama's warmth and love attracted everyone who met her. Oh, how I missed them!

I heard Daniel outside. He bounded into the dugout. "All the talk in town is about statehood and the vote that is coming soon."

"Yes, I'll miss it," I said. "New Mexico will become a state without me."

Daniel chuckled. "I'm sure they'll miss you too. By the way, the men in town said it'll take us several months to get to Nebraska."

"I don't think it will take several months, but it will take several weeks. We need to go slowly and stop each day in time to build camp before sundown."

Daniel returned to the yard. I could hear him talking to Charlie, as he packed the wagons. "Help me put down the mattress and spread out the quilts here. There, I reckon that will give Ma a soft place to lie down. We'll roll up the rest."

"Patricia and Petey can sleep with Ma in this wagon," he explained. "The rest of us will sleep on the ground between the wagons using some of these blankets we've rolled up as bedrolls." Clearly, Daniel was embracing his role as the man of the family.

We had bought a couple of small Murphy wagons from other settler families desperate for cash. Daniel was pleased that the wagons came with side barrels for water and food boxes. They were good quality and still in fine shape except that we had to buy a spare wheel and axle, which normally came as regular equipment. The spares had been needed by the families in their treks to New Mexico. We had traveled by train from Oklahoma, a far easier journey. But now we were going to travel the only way we could afford.

"But I don't want to sleep on the ground," Charlie whined.

"Don't make things any harder than they already are!" Daniel snapped.

"Why can't I sleep in the wagon, too?" Charlie started to cry. "There's room right there." He sniffed through his tears. I imagined him pointing at an empty space about right for his skinny ten-year-old body.

Daniel sounded exasperated. "And where do you think other important things will go? Like the cooking pots, the table and chairs, Mother's rocking chair and the special wooden box with her papers and her books?" His voice dripped with condescension. "Now, go inside and see what else is ready to carry out."

Daniel worried about me and my health. I avoided telling him when my arthritis flared up because I didn't want to worry him too much. But he was observant and seemed to know anyway. Since Sam's death, I'd moved a little more easily because I'd been getting more sleep, but this long ride would not be easy.

I watched Petey lugging the cast iron skillet to the wagon. Daniel grinned and reached down to help. Petey, with his dark brown eyes and thick wavy hair, looked like me. The other boys took after their father—tall, handsome with blue eyes and straight dark hair.

"Thanks, Petey." Daniel put the skillet in the corner of the wagon where the cooking pots would go within easy reach. "Go ask Ma if there's something else you can carry out."

Daniel was fond of his little brother, who was frail and small for a four-year-old. I knew he worried about Petey, too, and how he'd fair on this long trip. After all, we'd almost lost Petey last year when he lay in a fever. For days, he was hot, limp and unresponsive. I was frantic with fear.

Sam had sent Daniel into town to get the doctor who came immediately. He told us Petey had rheumatic fever and that he would probably not survive. I prayed fervently that he would recover. I sat by his side. holding his hand and wiping his forehead with cool water. Finally, after several days, he woke up and asked for something to eat. For a long time, he was so weak, the boys had to carry him because he couldn't stand or walk. Now, despite being small, he looked healthy. Always happy, with a smile for everyone, he seemed to know how lucky he was.

While Daniel directed the younger boys, I packed the cedar box that Sam had made for me. I put in Mark Twain's Huckleberry Finn, a present from Sam when he returned from a trip to Phoenix, a book of Longfellow's poems and a couple of other books, the envelope with all of Sam's papers, and some lesson plans I used to teach the children.

I heard Daniel yelling at Joe. "Where have you been? You are supposed to be helping Ma inside. Go see what she needs you to pack."

Joe mumbled a response sounding something like "Feeding the cows." Then he yelled, "Don't tell me what to do!"

Poor Joe was doing his best. Two years younger than Daniel, he never quite met his older brother's expectations. I realized that I'd been remiss. I needed to give him more attention, especially since Sam was gone.

FIVE

❧

Reflections

May 1911

The wagons were loaded. Charlie was pouting when he climbed up next to Joe, who was driving the mules in the second wagon. Charlie had been reminded again that he couldn't sleep in the wagon and I guessed he was still mad at Daniel. Joe grinned widely and looked so happy and proud to take the reins that he was oblivious of Charlie's foul mood. Daniel helped me up to the back of the first wagon pulled by our two horses, Sally and Socks. After he climbed up at the front, Daniel called to the back of the wagon, "Ready, ho!"

"Ready, ho!" I responded. We began to move.

Petey, sitting with Daniel, yelled, "Goodbye dugout" as we eased away.

The wagons moved and I relaxed, feeling my trust in Daniel and comforted by his manly voice. I was relieved that this life was ending. But the relief left quickly as I thought of the challenges ahead.

I sat at the back of the wagon holding Patricia, and

as the wagon rolled down the road, I looked at the rocks, with the rough wooden door to the dugout that had served as our home and thought about the life I'd had here.

We had arrived in New Mexico almost two years earlier. During our first few weeks, Sam, helped by the older boys and a generous neighbor, dug out the hard dry soil in the mountainside. The work was grueling but, finally, they had prepared two rooms—one large, one small. They made adobe bricks to build up the walls around the entrance and to construct steps down into the large room. The neighbor had generously offered some leftover wood to build the entrance door.

The first time I stepped down into the dark coolness, the lantern cast shadows on the walls. There were no windows. It was not the house I imagined. "I feel like a bat in an underground cave," I told Sam.

But gradually I got used to it. I was grateful for the shelter it provided—cool in the summer, offering protection from the blistering sun. In the winter, it remained warm when the wind howled down the mountain. We'd planned to whitewash the walls but Patricia was born, and then Sam left to go on a trip to Phoenix. He was never well after that so the walls remained hard brown dirt.

I hung a quilt over the entrance to our small bedroom so we might have a little privacy. In the summer, we cooked and ate outside, and the boys slept on the ground. But in the cold weather, we all crowded into the main room. Our life was the same as most of our neighbors. Only those who had come to New Mexico several years ago had built adobe houses. Many others, those who couldn't find water, had simply given up and moved on.

The fall after we arrived in New Mexico, Sam and I had argued. I wanted the boys to go to school. But Sam didn't think it necessary.

"You're a teacher," he said. "Can't you teach them here? It would be easier than riding the six miles into town."

"They need to be around other children," I countered. "Daniel's old enough to watch over Joe and Charlie. If the weather's bad, I'll teach them at home just like I did in Oklahoma."

Sam gave in. Charlie went to the elementary school built by the town in 1902. Daniel and Joe started at the new Tucumcari high school, which had just opened the previous fall. I was proud of how well they did in school. Even Charlie could handle money and count his change at the mercantile when I needed him to buy supplies in town.

As we left the dugout behind, my reverie continued. I remembered vividly when the unexpected winter storm arrived late last fall. The boys had left for school on the horses after they'd done their chores, just as the Eastern sky was beginning to lighten. Daniel rode Socks and Joe and Charlie rode Sally. Petey, just four, stayed behind with me. Sam had left over ten days' earlier to go to Phoenix. He was supposed to be back after a week and I was getting worried that he hadn't yet returned.

I stayed busy with chores and caring for Patricia, who was just three months old then. The sky was cloudless and shimmered a deep blue in sharp contrast against the dark brown rocks surrounding our dugout. But by early after-noon, the sky began turning gray as clouds roiled across the sun. The clothes I had hung out to dry, snapped with the gusts of wind. Then the temperature started dropping quickly. Huge drops of rain splattered in the dust.

I called to Petey who was scrambling over the rocks, "Come down now and go inside. There's a storm coming." I began grabbing overalls and shirts, as the wind whirled the dirt, leaves and tumbleweeds. I was shocked when the raindrops turned to huge flakes of snow.

Where were the boys? It was past time they should be home from school. I squinted down the dirt path, trying to see beyond the swirling whiteness. Were those shadows moving on the horizon? Or were those dark silhouettes just rocks?

"Mama, hurry! Come inside." Petey cried from the dugout.

"I'll be right there. Don't worry." But I was worried. Frantic, really. What if the boys were lost? What could I do? I couldn't leave Petey and Patricia to look for them. And then, where was Sam? Perhaps he was caught in this storm, too.

I stared hard again down the path. Those dark silhouettes were moving! Relief flooded through me and I rushed down the steps inside the dugout with a load of clothes. I tripped on the bottom step and almost fell, but caught myself by grabbing the edge of the nearby table.

Petey was crying and asking for Daniel. I gave him a hug. "Daniel's coming." I said.

When I stepped outside again, I could make out Daniel, on Socks, bent low against the wind and blinding snow. He was leading Sally with the younger boys hunched down protectively over their horse.

I hobbled quickly back outside to get an armload of wood for the stove. They finally pushed their way into our yard. "Hi, Ma," Daniel said, smiling weakly.

I threw my arms around his shivering body, tears tumbling down my cheeks. "I'm so glad you made it! I was so worried"

"Oh, Ma, we were all right. The horses can find their way." Joe said, brushing off my concern. I hugged him and Charlie anyway to let them know how happy I was that they were safe. He and Charlie were both shaking from the cold, too.

Daniel began giving orders. "Charlie, help Ma carry the wood and go inside. Joe and I will tie up the horses in the shed and give them some hay."

When they stomped into the dugout and huddled around the stove for warmth, I watched as the intensity and fear melted off their faces. They gradually warmed up and their shivering and shaking slowed down.

"Why isn't Pa home?" Joe asked with a hint of scorn after we ate our supper of eggs and potatoes that evening. He seemed angry at Sam for going away again. I wondered if he resented the extra chores he needed to do.

I tried to look relaxed when I turned to answer. I didn't want him to see how worried I was. "I'm sure Dad is on his way. He'll be all right." Actually, I hadn't been able to eat much. My stomach was knotted up.

Sam had gone to Phoenix because there seemed to be some problem with his pension that he avoided telling me about. We were low on money and I knew he was fretting.

He'd left without warm clothes and the walk from the train station in Tucumcari was six miles.

"Don't worry," said Daniel, giving me a reassuring hug. "Pa will make it home before it gets much colder."

I fretted all evening imagining Sam freezing to death. All that night, I sat up by the stove crocheting while the children slept.

The next day, with the wind howling and more snow beginning to fall, Daniel went out to feed the animals. I heard him yell. Joe rushed outside. I waited in the dugout, dreading what I might see out there. A couple of minutes later, he and Daniel helped Sam down the ladder into the dugout. They were practically carrying him. He could barely stand on his feet. The snow in his hair and beard had turned to ice. His clothes were rigid and frozen. His fingers were stiff and frostbitten. His eyes were unfocused and he shook violently all over, mumbling sounds none of us could understand.

Daniel and Joe removed his stiff and frozen clothes and carried him to bed. I piled extra quilts on him to warm him up. For the next few days, he was incoherent, muttering words that made no sense. I sat with him holding his hand and pouring warm liquids down him. I prayed that he would recover.

I was thankful that after a few days, he seemed to feel better. But my relief was short-lived when he came down with a fever and a deep racking cough. The cough hung on for weeks and I worried that he would never be healthy.

Despite his long recovery, Sam was happy. "Hey, my sweet, I'm getting my pension!" he exclaimed when he was finally better. He picked me up in a big hug. I looked up at him, smiling. I was reassured that he was finally acting like himself again. He laughed and teased the boys as they did the chores, played with the baby, gave me frequent hugs and told stories of his trip to Phoenix to resolve his pension.

One evening after the New Year, Sam had complained, "Why is it so hot in here?" But it wasn't the dugout, he had a fever again. He soon became delirious, repeating my name and claiming he hadn't been married before. I had hoped to find out what he was talking about, but now I would never know what had disturbed him.

I had never wanted to leave Nebraska and my family. But ten years ago, Sam had begun promoting a move to Oklahoma. I refused to consider it.

He sulked and pestered me. I reluctantly gave in. I knew it would make him happy. But, after a few years, I grew to like our place in Oklahoma. There was a spring with cool fresh water and a small stream that flowed from it. I loved my garden there. Daniel figured out how to direct the water from the stream to irrigate the garden to help it flourish in the hot weather. The summer sun was unrelenting, the heat shimmering on the dirt road. But the house stayed cool from the shade of the cottonwood tree and with the doors and windows open, the breeze cooled things even more.

In contrast, the winters were cold and the doctor had urged Sam to move to a climate with warmer winters for his asthma. He had traveled to Dallas and to Phoenix and spent three different winters there, leaving me alone with the children. Initially, I'd felt pretty lonely and abandoned, but, fortunately, we had neighbors nearby who were helpful when Sam was away, so I didn't feel totally alone. My confidence increased and I was less fearful after his second trip.

Sometimes, when it rained in Oklahoma, the water gushed from the sky and produced flash floods. I told the children to stay out of the streambeds and gullies. In contrast, in New Mexico, we had no water and had to buy it by the barrel from the lucky ones who'd found water when they drilled wells. I had to get after the boys at first but they quickly learned to use the water sparingly.

Sam's asthma had not improved during his winters away and he came home one day with a notice about the millions of acres of government land surrounding Tucumcari, New Mexico, that were free to anyone who would settle on the land.

"Look, Sarah, it is just like the other homestead laws. All we need to do is live on it for five years to get our 160 acres."

"But Sam, I don't want to move again. I like our neighbors here."

Sam acted like he didn't hear me. "This here description says that the 'clean air is good for asthma'. That's good. Doc wants me to move to a climate warmer than here."

Of course, that circular didn't mention that there wasn't even enough rain to grow pole beans. Sam was tantalized with the possibilities and I didn't want to hold him back. With the hope of finding a farming paradise, a warmer climate and improving Sam's health, we sold our land, horses and livestock, packed up and joined hundreds of other settlers heading west.

Finding water had been our biggest challenge. Even the railroad had drilled several wells before they found water. Several of the neighbors had drilled multiple useless wells. On our homestead, Sam had paid for two trials without success. But our money from the sale of our homestead in Oklahoma was running out and Sam hadn't heard about his pension. So we had decided to wait until the next year to try again. Once a week, like many others, the boys went into town to buy a barrel of water.

Now, as we traveled towards Nebraska, I didn't have to worry about drilling for water. But, I had plenty of other concerns.

Before we left, I sent a letter to the government to request the information about the benefits for widows. They sent forms and I filled them out and sent them back right away. I had even sent them a postcard letting them know I was moving back to Nebraska. I needed that money for us to live on.

SIX

❧

The Perilous Journey Home

Daniel and I had planned the first leg of our trip togeth-er guided by the availability of water. We planned to spend the first night in Hudson about a day's ride away and the largest place between Tucumcari and Logan. We had heard about a Mrs. Rice who had a store that was a major trading center in Hudson that had the only well in the vi-cinity. Hudson was near the Texas border and we could then follow the Canadian River across the Panhandle of Texas, into Oklahoma Territory and then head north.

Daniel had learned in town about crossing the Canadian River at Plemons' Crossing, in the Texas Panhandle, where the river was supposedly shallow and we could get help from the river guides to avoid the quicksand bogs. I thought it would take us about ten days to get to Plemons' Crossing.

Now I felt the wagon slow and stop.

Then Daniel's smiling face, soft dark whiskers begin-ning to cover his upper lip, appeared at the back of the wag-on. I was resting on the mattress that he had prepared for me and dozed off with the rhythm of the swaying wagon.

Patricia nestled next to me. I sat up slowly, feeling each of my joints release the tightness as I pushed myself upright.

"Are we in Hudson?" I asked.

"Yeah, Ma. Thought you'd want to get out and stretch before we pulled up to the store."

He knew my descent from the wagon would be awkward and didn't want to embarrass me by having me do it in front of strangers. I appreciated his thoughtfulness. As I handed Patricia to him, he blew a kiss under her chin, producing a smile and giggles in response. I climbed out backward carefully, putting a foot on each of the wooden steps, Daniel gently guiding my feet to each one and then onto the stool he'd set on the ground. We had stopped on the edge of town, the rutted road continued on between the two rows of adobe buildings.

"I'll walk with Patricia to stretch out," I said. "Bring the wagons along after I get to the store."

Settling Patricia on my left hip, I took a deep breath to quiet my anxiety, and started toward the store. I walked slowly, but as my right hip loosened up, I could feel my gait smooth out. On the left side stood a saloon, the post office, the Rice General Store and a couple of other low buildings. Another store, a saloon, and what might be a boarding house lined the opposite side of the street.

Behind the store, several wagons and tents were set up in an empty area with a barbed wire fence on two sides. One rough wooden fencepost was attached to the store, the other to an adobe building with a canvas roof and partitions inside that might be stalls for horses, mules and oxen. And there in the middle of the yard stood the prize pump.

A few men had gathered in front of the saloon across from the Rice General Store arguing, and gesturing wildly. I was nervous to walk past these strangers with their loud voices and aggressive postures. As I approached, the men stopped arguing and stared with curiosity but their greetings were friendly and they tipped their hats with a "Howdy, Ma'am." I responded with "Good evening" and a smile. I knew acutely that an unknown woman alone would create a stir. I assumed that they would just wonder who I was and leave me alone.

The store was dark inside and I paused to let my eyes adjust before I dared make my way across the earthen floor. When I found my bearings and proceeded, my shoes crunched on the hard dirt as I stepped gingerly toward a counter in the back. A tall heavy-set woman stood behind the counter. She had iron gray hair and several strands hung from the bun at the crown of her head. Her eyelids drooped over gray eyes and her face was wrinkled from a life outside in the sun and wind. Her dress and apron were threadbare and faded. The deep creases around her mouth were turned down into a grimace. She looked down at me with a hard unwelcoming stare.

"You must be Mrs. Rice?" I smiled and held out my hand. A puzzled frown distorted her face as if she were trying to place me.

"I'm Mrs. Martin, from Tucumcari. I'm recently widowed and taking my five children back home to Nebraska. Might we stay the night out back?"

At that moment, Patricia's whimpering became loud crying, as if she were announcing her fear of this woman and the dark room with its tall stacks of goods and narrow aisles. We were surrounded by strange odors—of leather, spices and dried meat, mixed with the scents of people who hadn't washed for days or weeks. I comforted her, speaking softly, patting her back and swaying back and forth. Mrs. Rice glared and said nothing. It was as if she had never seen a small child cry.

When Patricia settled, Mrs. Rice finally responded. "Yeah, I'm Mrs. Rice, Clara Rice. And you can stay if you can pay. It's twenty-five cents for hay for the animals and twenty-five for the wagon and—"

"Yes, of course, we will pay," I interrupted. She was a rather frightening woman and I was anxious to get out of there. "We have two wagons and we'll also want a barrel of water."

"OK, a dollar fifty then," she barked.

"Thank you." I kept our money in a kerchief in my bosom. I turned away to get it out, then turned back to hand her six quarters. "Thank you very much."

Once outside, I took a deep breath of relief and walked back to our wagons. "I paid up," I told Daniel. "We can stay behind the store."

He and Joe moved the wagons. While they tended the animals, Charlie helped me by getting the pot from the wagon and filling it with water to start the beans.

"Thanks, Charlie for being so helpful," I said. He beamed at me and then ran to ferry two cups of flour from the wagon to the mixing bowl for the biscuits.

When Daniel returned from the animal shed, he helped by tending the beans, flavoring them with a small piece of the salt pork. When everything was ready, Joe helped dish up a plate of beans and a biscuit for everyone. My chest was bursting with pride for my boys. "Thank you for being so helpful," I said.

That night, with the boys bedded down between the two wagons, I felt the warmth of Patricia at my side and heard Petey's breathing from under the blanket next to me. Now that they were all asleep, I allowed myself to think ahead. I longed for Sam's strength. Instead, I turned to prayer for comfort.

"Dear God," I said aloud, "Give me strength and guidance." It had been a long first day. I was exhausted. It wasn't long before I fell asleep.

"Come back here! That's ours!"

I woke with a start, jarred out of a deep sleep. I rolled away from the sleeping Patricia and leaned out over the edge of the wagon to peek out. In the light of the moon, I could see Daniel wrestling with a figure. I yelled, "Get out of here!" The man wrenched himself from Daniel's grasp, and, holding something under his arm, he ran off into the night. Daniel took off after him, disappearing into the dark before I could even call to him to be careful.

After about ten minutes he returned with a gunny sack—it looked like the flour or the potatoes—and put it back into the second wagon.

"Damned thief!" he muttered, breathing heavily as he brushed himself off. "Thought he could get away with taking our food… like we was easy pickin's!"

"Are you all right?" My heart was thumping wildly.

"Just mad. That guy was hanging out across the road

from the store yesterday afternoon. I didn't like his looks. Now I know why! Damn him! I got our potatoes but he took the salt pork and a skillet!"

I was beginning to calm down. "Well, we just won't have as much meat as we had planned." I wanted to reassure him despite my concern. "We can get by."

Joe and Charlie were cowering under the wagon. "Hey boys, it's OK. Relax. He's gone."

"Thank the Lord you weren't hurt and that he didn't get anything else. You did great, son." I realized again that this trip was not going to be an easy one.

Ten days later...

As we began our descent from the high plains Daniel and Joe carefully pulled the ropes controlling the break levers to stop the wagons from running away downhill. As I rode at the front of the first wagon I gasped at the beauty of the canyon in front of us. The river had sculpted a deep gorge through the layers of rock, glowing in shades of red, orange, tan, and magenta set off by the azure sky. I wondered if the river was really red or whether it was a reflection of the canyon walls. The short brush and green trees on the shore added another vivid contrast. But hidden underneath all that beauty was the treachery of the rocks, rushing water and deceptive quicksand bogs.

We were close to Plemon's Crossing where we planned to stop for supplies and information before setting up camp to prepare to cross the river. I could see the cluster of buildings in the distance as we descended the steep and windy road. Here, the Canadian River was wide and shallow. I hoped it would offer us an easy wagon crossing.

We agreed that Daniel and the boys would stay outside the general store with the wagons, while I went inside. As Daniel jumped down and came around the wagon to help me down, I saw him eyeing two farmers who were talking close by. As I started for the store, I heard one of them say, "Howdy, son. You're not from these parts are you?" I looked back, noticing that the taller of the two had a friendly, almost fatherly appearance.

"No sir. We're from New Mexico," Daniel said. I sensed he didn't want to reveal too much information to strangers, probably remembering the man who stole our food and supplies.

"Where ya headed?" The other farmer was a short pudgy man chewing on a long piece of grass. His eyes narrowed as he spoke.

Daniel stepped back, took a breath and stood taller. "We're headin' to Nebraska. What can you tell me about crossing the Canadian here?" I continued to stand on the other side of the wagon and listen. "Well, young man, you should cross here at Plemons. Best crossing in the Panhandle." the tall man replied. "Veer to the left on the other side and you won't need to pay Barney to take you across—"

"Oh I don't know," the short man interrupted. "Them quicksand bogs is pretty fickle and moves around."

"Yeah, they can be treacherous," the tall man said, "but if you be sure you keep your team to the left of the tree growing out of the rock on the other side, you can do it. Otherwise, you'll sink your wheels up to the axle and you can't get out without help."

"Be sure yah check it out before you take the wagons over," the short man suggested. "Don't count on them bogs bein' in the same place tomorrow that they was today."

As the conversation concluded, I proceeded into the store, approaching the man behind the counter with a smile. Holding out my hand, I said in the strongest voice I could muster, "Hello, sir. I am Mrs. Martin, taking my children back to Nebraska after my husband's death in New Mexico."

The man's round face broke into a grin that held at least two missing teeth. "Glad to meet yah, Mrs. Martin. Sorry to hear about your husband. I'm James Jones, but they just call me Jones."

"How do you do, Mr. Jones."

"Just Jones, ma'am. How can I help you?"

"I need some supplies and some wax to seal our wagons to cross the river. What can you tell me about crossing the Canadian here?" I, too, was reluctant to reveal how vulnerable we were.

Jones grinned again, and although his face relaxed his eyes were observing me intently. "Well, a little woman like you… if you don't have no man to help pull you out if you get stuck in the quicksand, I reckon you need to hire Barney Plemons. He's got a horse that has an uncanny sense of where them damn bogs are. He can guide your team and wagons across so as to miss 'em. Them bogs is pretty dangerous… they move from one day to the next. Can't be sure that the route you figure out one day will be safe the next. The bad thing is he charges a small fortune.

But in your case, it's probably worth it. The last wagon that tried to cross—"

I interrupted him not really wanting to know about the last wagon. "How much?"

"Don't let him charge you any more than three bits a wagon and team," Jones warned. "That last wagon didn't want to pay and went across without Barney. Hit one of those bogs that looked solid. Turned out it wasn't and they went in up to the axle. They was lucky 'cause those bogs can swallow the wagon, team and all, in minutes. That guy was cocky. Thought he could handle it. Ended up having to pay twice as much to get pulled out."

"What happens if you hit one of those bogs when Mr. Plemons is guiding you?" I asked.

"Oh, don't you worry your pretty little head about that," Jones soothed. "Barney'll pull you out."

I tried to smile politely, but I was annoyed at his efforts to sweet talk me. "Thank you, Jones." I was trying to be firm. "I want to talk to Mr. Plemons. Where can I find him?"

"When do you want to cross?"

"Tomorrow, if he is available. We have a long way to go. Need to keep moving every day."

"I'll tell him you need him tomorrow. He'll be at the river in the mornin'."

"Thank you, Jones. I appreciate your help."

SEVEN

Preparing to Cross

I tried to put all the crossing's potential hazards out of my mind as I skinned the rabbits that Daniel had caught for supper. The horses and mules were tethered on the other side of the wagons. The younger boys had gathered some dead brush and branches to get the fire started. Then they headed off to pick some berries they had seen growing near the river. Daniel had put the cook pot over the fire to heat water for rabbit stew. Good that Daniel caught the rabbit since we didn't have any salt pork now. Potatoes and a few wild onions would add flavor.

Petey was playing with Patricia, tossing her a small round rock he was using like a ball. She giggled with delight and would say "ag'in" after he rolled it toward her as she sat on the blanket. She was learning a few words with the boys' encouragement.

Daniel came around the wagon leading Socks. "Ma, I am going to check out the river and the quicksand. Be back for supper," he called as he mounted his horse.

I flashed with anger. "There's no need for you to take that risk. We're going to hire Mr. Plemons to guide us tomorrow." Daniel ignored me and guided Socks toward the river. "Daniel, come back here!" I yelled after him.

He was just like his father. It was useless to try to stop him when he got his mind set on something. He had agreed with me that we needed to be extra cautious when we talked after the incident in Hudson. But he was young and wanted to prove he was a man. But he was still a boy when he took these risks. I guessed he wanted to figure out where the quicksand was, maybe hoping we wouldn't need a guide and could save money. Still, I was annoyed that he didn't listen.

Joe and Charlie were back with a basket filled with juicy berries so dark they almost looked black. I smiled as I noticed the smears across their faces revealing what happened to those that didn't make it into the basket. After they set the basket down, they too started down the path to the river. When I asked where they were going, Charlie responded, "Joe says the water is cool and we can get cleaned up."

"Be careful," I hollered and then chuckled as I heard Joe say, "It will feel so good. We haven't had a bath since we left New Mexico. I'm surprised Ma hasn't told us we smell."

A few minutes later, I heard a scream. It was Joe. "Ma! Ma! A snake!"

"Petey, stay with your sister!" I yelled, rushing toward the river. Joe was running back up the path toward me, hollering that it was Charlie. "Get a knife and a cloth from the wagon," I yelled. When I reached him, I practically threw Charlie on the ground, ordered him to lay still and examined his right leg.

"Whew!" I took a deep breath. There were no puncture marks on this leg, just a deep scratch about an inch long from the brush. I looked at his left leg. It too was smooth. I said a prayer of gratitude.

"Where did you see this snake?" I asked.

"Over there, behind those rocks." Charlie pointed gingerly.

"Well, you're lucky. That snake was just as afraid of you as you were of it," I teased. "You just have a scratch from the brush there. That's what you felt. You were so afraid you thought it was a snake bite."

"Is it safe to go in the water?" Charlie stammered, his eyes darting from me to the water.

"Come on in," hollered Joe, who was already standing knee-deep in the water. "It feels good. Just stay away from the rocks up there, where the snakes hang out." Charlie cautiously climbed over a log toward the river.

"Joe, be careful and look out for your brother, please. I need to go back. Petey's alone watching Patricia." I looked across the river for Daniel. I could see a dark form moving back and forth. My anger flared again at his disobedience, but it was immediately replaced by worry. I decided to talk to him about contradicting me like this. Then I turned to go back to the fire and cooking supper.

In the gray light of the early dawn the next morning, I got up slowly to let my joints wake up. I stirred the fire and set a small pot of water on for my tea. The children were still sleeping so I had a few moments of prayerful silence. Remembering my angry conversation with Daniel last night about his disobedience and his disagreement over hiring Barney Plemons, I asked forgiveness. I also asked for God's help to safely cross the river. Then I repeated a line from Rudyard Kipling, "Lord God of Hosts, be with us yet, Lest we forget—lest we forget!"

The children were beginning to wake, sleepily climbing out of their quilts, when I noticed a horseman coming over the rise toward our camp. "That must be Mr. Plemons," I said.

Daniel was helping Petey get on his shoes and, as he looked up, his glance caught my eye. I relaxed feeling my appreciation of his support and concern. When I smiled at him, his face lit up with a wide grin. Our disagreement was over.

I took a few short steps toward the approaching figure. With the rising sun at his back, I couldn't make out his face until he pulled up next to me. Then, I saw a man about my age with warm brown eyes and an easy smile. He was riding a handsome horse, black as tar with a brilliant white spot on his forehead.

"Good morning! Mr. Plemons?"

He removed his hat, "Yes, ma'am, Barney Plemons, at your service. Jones told me you might need help getting across the river this mornin'. Them quicksand bogs is pretty tricky."

"When I checked last evenin'," Daniel said, his tone defiant, "we could go just left of the tree that grows out the rock on the other side. We don't need your help."

"Hello son," Plemons said, turning towards Daniel. "Plemons, here."

"I'm sorry… where are my manners?" I said. "I'm Mrs. Sarah Martin and this is my son Daniel."

"Pleased to meet ya, Mrs. Martin. Jones had told me the name was Martin. Howdy Daniel."

Daniel walked up to shake hands.

As Plemons took his hand, he said, "Son, ya must have been talking to Jack Cook. He always tells everybody to go that route. Trouble is, bogs change from one day to the next. What looked good yesterday can be a trap today. If you checked out the left of the tree yesterday, it might not be safe today."

Plemons turned to me. "The last wagon that tried to cross without our help got stuck in one of those bogs, you could lose the team, wagon and all your children in just a few minutes."

"So how do you know what way is safe, Mr. Plemons?" Daniel demanded.

Plemons grinned. "Son, I don't know what way is safe. It's Ezekiel here that knows." He fondly patted the glistening neck of his horse. "He's a special horse that has an extra sense about those bogs."

Daniel snorted. "A horse with special sense! What happens if the horse is wrong and we get stuck in the quicksand?"

I shot Daniel a look to back off. Then I smiled at Mr. Plemons. "We would like your help, please, sir. I don't want to take any chances with my family. What do you charge?"

"I need a buck for each wagon here to help pay for my time and for Ezekiel here."

I remembered that Jones had cautioned to not agree

to any more than seventy-five cents a wagon.

"Ah, Mr. Plemons," I said, using what Sam had called my "sweet honey voice"—the voice he said would get me anything I wanted. "I'm a widow taking my five children back to my family's place in Nebraska. Now I know you need to feed your horse and that you wouldn't take advantage of us. But I can only offer you seventy-five cents for each wagon. I think that is a fair price. I would be grateful if you and Ezekiel would accept that and guide us safely across." I gave him the sweetest smile I could muster.

Plemons touched his hat. "Why ma'am, Ezekiel and I would be honored to guide you across for a buck fifty." Daniel had walked back toward the wagons, shaking his head but he turned to watch as I continued the negotiation.

"And, I'm sure, Mr. Plemons, included in your fee," I said, smiling up at him, "is help in getting us out, if, for some reason, we do get caught in one of those unseen bogs. I'm sure you can give us that assurance because you have confidence in your horse Ezekiel, right?"

"Yes, ma'am." As Plemons spoke, I saw Daniel duck his head to hide the smile that had begun to spread across his face. Maybe Daniel wouldn't feel so resistant to my decision now.

"Gives us a little time, here, Mr. Plemons," I said. "We need to get the wagons ready. And I want to be sure all the children are ready, too. Would you like a cup of tea while you wait?"

While Plemons drank his tea, Charlie and Joe waxed the cracks of the wagons to keep the water out and I packed up our pans and supplies. Daniel tied down our belongings, wrapped the bed rolls, and put my box of papers on top of a bag of clothes to be sure it stayed dry. Then he tied our big tarps tightly over both wagons. We were ready.

EIGHT

The Quicksand Bog

Now, Mrs. Martin," Mr. Plemons said as we stood at the riverbank, "you and the young ones'll stay here until Daniel and I get the wagons across. Me and Ezekiel'll take the lead. Daniel'll walk beside the horses, pulling the first wagon to keep them calm. The mules with the second wagon will follow. Once across, Daniel'll stay with the wagons and the mules. I'll come back with the horses to get you and the children loaded up and lead you across."

Daniel opened his mouth; it looked as if he were about to object but I jumped in. "Daniel, when you get across, will you make sure the bedding didn't get wet and lay anything out to dry if need be? I'm especially concerned that my box stays dry."

"Of course, Ma. I know that." He seemed to grudgingly accept the direction from Mr. Plemons.

Joe then turned to plead his case. "Ma, why can't I go over with Daniel and Mr. Plemons? I can make sure the mules follow. Please."

"No Joe. I want you here."

"Actually, he has a good idea," Plemons spoke up. "If

you want him to help get the small children across, he can come back with me." Plemons was right. I agreed and Joe was thrilled.

I sat on a large rock, holding Patricia, as I intently watched Socks and Sally pull the first wagon into the river. Daniel walked alongside, reassuring the horses as they strained against the force of the water.

The river was shallow but rocks and boulders covered the bottom, some protruding above the water. The current was swift and Plemons had told us that the rocks under the water were slippery with moss. As the wheels slipped over them, and the wagons shuddered and lurched. The mules followed reluctantly with the second wagon. Joe walked beside them, snapping the whip above their heads to prod them along.

I sat very still and had to remind myself to breathe. Patricia must have sensed my concern because she didn't move either. Initially, Daniel slipped on the rocks frequently, catching his balance before he took another step. As he reached the center of the river he seemed to have found his footing, pushing against the current to keep upright. I began to relax, but suddenly he disappeared into the rapidly moving water. I leapt to my feet.

As I watched helplessly from the bank, I was shaking so much that Patricia began to howl. I saw Daniel's head rise above the water, then he vanished again. I gasped for air, fearing the worst. Then I caught sight of his thrashing arms. Why couldn't he find his footing? As he struggled, he, the horses, wagon were drifting downstream. Joe snapped the whip above the mules, trying to prevent them from following.

Then abruptly Daniel stood up and, with a shake of his head, cleared the water from his face. He waved at me as if to say he was alright then proceeded onward, shouting encouragement to the horses. I took a few deep breaths to stop my shaking, hugged Patricia, and sat down.

For a while, Charlie sat on the ground with Petey, transfixed by the swaying wagons as they heaved and rolled across the river. But, after the novelty wore off, they began to entertain themselves by throwing pebbles into the water. I smiled, happy to see them having fun. They were so distracted that they missed Daniel's fall into the river.

As I continued to watch the slow progress of the wagons I noticed the horses veer to the right. It looked like they were trying to take a shorter route toward the river bank. Again, I stood up with alarm. What was Daniel doing? Socks seemed to be struggling. Was he caught in quicksand? Mr. Plemons gestured and yelled at Daniel, although with the noise of the water rushing over the rocks I couldn't hear what he said.

Daniel snapped the whip at Socks, apparently in an effort to right their direction, but it had little effect and they continued to head away from Ezekiel. Mr. Plemons yelled and pointed in the opposite direction. Daniel cracked the whip again and Socks seemed to stumble and pause. Then, regaining his footing, Socks finally turned to follow Ezekiel again. I swallowed and let out my breath as I watched the whole party pull up on the river bank on the other side.

Daniel unhitched the horses and handed the halter ropes to Mr. Plemons so he could lead the horses back across the river. Then Daniel tethered the mules. Joe hopped up on Socks. I hoped Daniel was using his manners to thank Mr. Plemons for everything he'd done.

When Plemons got back to where we waited, I climbed up on Sally, the gentler of the two horses. I'd bound Patricia to my chest with the length of cloth I used to hold her whenever I needed two hands. Petey sat behind me, hugging my waist, bouncing up and down with excitement. Joe had Charlie in front of him on Socks. I caught Joe's eye and thanked him for keeping the mules in check. He grinned.

"We will all do just fine with Mr. Plemons guiding us," I said, as much to reassure myself as the children.

"Are we all ready to head out?" Mr. Plemons asked as he led the horses around two big boulders at the edge of the river.

I looked across the river, searching for Daniel. I spotted him and waved. "Yes, sir," I said. "Let's go." As we made our way into the swiftly moving water, Daniel waved and yelled, but I couldn't hear what he said. I looked over at Joe and Charlie. Charlie was holding onto Joe as tight as he could. The next time I looked across the river, Daniel had disappeared from sight.

I focused on watching Ezekiel picking his way around large rocks and boulders. Joe urged the reluctant Socks to follow. "Be careful, Joe, especially in the deepest part of the river," I yelled to him. The water was now up around my knees. I needed all my attention not to panic. I was grateful that Mr. Plemons and Ezekiel were guiding us.

Petey was still bouncing around. I hollered over my

shoulder, "Petey, be a good boy and sit still."

When we were about two-thirds of the way across I relaxed a little. Sally was a comfortable easy horse and she carefully placed each foot before she moved forward. On the other side of the river I saw the wagons, with the quilt and some clothes drying on the bushes, but still no Daniel. I reassured myself that he must be resting nearby. I couldn't worry about him now. Sally continued her careful plodding.

Suddenly, Plemons dropped the harness ropes and Ezekiel took off, lunging toward the bank upriver. It was then that I saw Daniel. His head and neck just visible above the sand at the edge of the river. He was caught in a quick-sand bog, his arms flailing as he struggled to get out.

My heart pounded wildly. I gripped the reins tightly and pulled back to signal Sally to stop and wait. I watched as Mr. Plemons deftly threw the rope to Daniel who grabbed at it and missed. Plemons pulled the rope back and again whirled it around is head and threw it to Daniel. This time, he caught it and held on. The horse and rider moved backward slowly. Daniel lost his hold and slipped backward.

I glanced at Joe and Charlie. Their eyes were wide and their mouths hung open. I was holding my breath. Plemons tried again. This time, Daniel not only caught the rope, but he also managed to put it over his head and shove it down under his arms. Again, Ezekiel gracefully moved backward. Daniel held firm to the rope around his chest. Finally, the suction of the sand and water that had captured him broke. When I saw him stumble up onto the bank a short way upriver, I said a prayer of thanks.

"Joe, get Socks up on the river bank," I said. Sally followed Socks. I waited for Joe to come over to take Patricia so I could also dismount. I moved slowly. My joints were very stiff. My anxiety didn't help. Charlie jumped down from Socks and came over to help Petey.

Then, Mr. Plemons rode up on Ezekiel. "Ma'am, it's downright lucky that we was so close to this side or you might've lost your oldest son."

Tears filled my eyes. "Yes, sir. I am much obliged that you acted so quickly. I give you and Ezekiel my thanks and appreciation."

A contrite Daniel, covered in wet sand, finally made his way down the river. He stumbled and sat down on a large boulder, staring at the ground avoiding my eyes.

But Joe confronted him. "Daniel, how could you be so dumb?"

"I was just looking around for a place for us to camp," he replied.

We needed to discuss this more, but now was not the time. I needed to take charge.

"Daniel, you go behind that boulder over there," I said. "Be sure there are no bogs. Wash out your clothes and put them out to dry." Despite my anger, I tried not to raise my voice. "Charlie, you watch Patricia. Joe, find a shirt and overalls for Daniel in the wagon. I need to sit and rest for a moment." I collapsed on a log and took a deep breath.

After a few minutes, I turned to Mr. Plemons. "Thank you again for your help. If you can wait just a bit, I will get you paid."

After my breathing became regular and I felt calmer, I retrieved some coins from the hiding place where I kept my money, adding a little extra to show my appreciation.

"No ma'am," Plemons protested as I handed the money to him. "I won't take the extra two bits. You need it." To my surprise, he handed it back to me, wheeled around on his horse, and galloped back to the river.

NINE

❦

The Intruder in Oklahoma

We camped an extra day on the north side of the Canadian, giving the horses and the mules time to recover from their exertion. Daniel was agreeable and helpful, doing extra chores to make up for his foolishness in getting trapped by the quicksand. I knew he was contrite and embarrassed so I didn't see any need to punish him. But I was still angry.

One evening around the fire, soon after we'd turned north from the Canadian River and headed toward the Oklahoma Panhandle, I decided to take the opportunity to talk to him again. I didn't want to scare the younger children so I waited until they had fallen asleep.

"Daniel, I want to remind you about how vulnerable we are out here on the prairie traveling without Pa. There's not only the risk of one of us getting seriously hurt. We could have lost you in that quicksand."

He shrugged as if to dismiss what I was saying.

Annoyed, I paused for a moment before continuing. "We're also potential victims to outlaws." I waited for his response. He looked down.

"You're a great help and I appreciate all that you do. I'm counting on you. But I can't afford for anything to happen to you."

His posture stiffened. "I'm a man now, Ma. I can take care of you and the children."

I knew he understood that I was concerned but maybe he didn't understand why.

"Do you know the history of Oklahoma Territory?"

Daniel shook his head, looking at me blankly.

I decided to tell him. "Before statehood was granted to Oklahoma in 1907, just four years ago, there was no government and no law enforcement in the Panhandle, so it was a pretty lawless place. It was called 'No man's land.' The government had moved reluctant tribes of Indians into this wild land. There was hostility between cattlemen from Texas and the 'nesters' which is what the pioneer settlers and farmers were called."

"But, didn't we live on a farm in Oklahoma. I thought Petey was born here. I don't remember it being wild and scary," Daniel said.

"Yes, we did. When your father talked about moving to Oklahoma in 1901 after Charlie was born, your Uncle Robert tried to discourage him. But your father was determined. Thank goodness we settled further east in Dewey County. It wasn't wild and ungoverned like the Panhandle. That place was inhabited by robbers, horse thieves and other riffraff known to hang out at the saloons in small communities along the trail."

Daniel's eyes were wide. "Is it still like that?"

"No, in the last few years, there have been more

settlements as the railroads have brought people into small communities, and more farmers move in to homestead. They don't drive cattle north anymore so the fights between the 'nesters' and cattlemen are over. More people and settlements meant lawmen and tough deputy marshals got elected."

"Whew! You had me worried." Daniel seemed relieved.

"Well, the reputation of the Territory's past still gnaws at the back of my mind," I confessed. "As I said earlier, we are vulnerable to someone who wants to take advantage of us."

"Oh Ma. We'll be all right." He was trying to reassure me.

Three Days Later...

We were all crowded in one wagon. It had been raining for two days and now it was pounding on the tarp we had rigged over us. We had stopped early because the horses were having a hard time pulling the wagon through the deep red mud. It was as slippery and soggy as bread dough. It was too wet to start a fire, so I'd served up some cold cornmeal left over from the previous night's supper. We fell asleep soon after supper, but it wasn't long until I woke with a start.

The wagon shuddered and lurched to one side. The horses were snorting as they jerked against their halter ropes. Beside me, Daniel sat up, pulled on his boots and grabbed his rifle. He peered outside then soundlessly climbed out the back.

"Be careful," I whispered., peering out after him. I saw a male figure trying to mount Socks. But Socks resisted, dancing around, not about to allow this stranger on his back.

"Halt! Or I'll shoot!" Daniel yelled as he raised his rifle. The man whirled around, dropping something to the ground and raising his hands beside his head. When the sky lit up with a flash of lightning, I saw a wild and unkempt figure, his eyes darting between Daniel and the horse. His hair was matted, his heavy beard ragged and his clothes tattered. He growled with a guttural, almost inhuman sound. Then, he leaped and kicked the rifle out of Daniel's hands. He and Daniel both dove after it in the mud.

"Oh no," I gasped. The man had grabbed the rifle and lifted it as if to knock Daniel in the head with the butt. Daniel rolled away and jumped up, lunged at the gun and managed to grab it and yank it away.

"Get out of here," he roared. "Move away from the wagon." Then, in a calmer tone he added, "Walk slowly over to the road."

The man stood his ground, growling like an animal again. I could feel my heart beating in my throat. Charlie and Joe were awake now. They were huddled up next to me.

Daniel took a step toward the intruder and yelled "I said move!"

Finally, the man began moving toward the road, making growling noises with each step.

"OK, now turn around and walk away," Daniel commanded. "I don't want to find you near us again. You hear me?"

The man turned slowly, taking uncertain steps and finally headed down the road, slipping in the mud as he went. He kept turning around as if to check if Daniel was still there.

"Good riddance!" Daniel yelled after him.

After the intruder had disappeared, he came over to reassure me. "Everything is fine now, Ma." He was breathing heavily. He was wet and muddy and smelled of his sweat. As he stowed the rifle, his hands shook.

Still, despite his fear, he'd been very brave in confronting the intruder. My son was becoming a man.

Daniel climbed back into the wagon, took off his muddy jacket, leaned back against a sack of flour. Soon his rhythmic breathing signaled that he was asleep. I was wide awake, worrying and listening to the children breathing. As I did so, I whispered a thankful prayer for my eldest son.

Still, I missed Sam and his reassurance. I remembered how he had gotten us to safety in Oklahoma when a storm came up and a flash flood threatened to tip over our wagon. He carried Charlie who was four, helped me, pregnant with Petey, and gave direction to Joe and Daniel. We clamored up a steep bank watching the water rise. We were worried about the horses and the wagon, but without our weight, the horses were able to pull the wagon out of the water and head home to the barn. Sam had been such a comfort. I felt empty now without him next to me.

The thunder was more distant now and the rain spattered gently on the tarp. Maybe it was letting up. I looked forward to getting to Beaver the next day, getting some supplies and drying things out. We'd be safer in town, too. Feeling more hopeful, I finally dozed off. When I awoke, I looked outside to see that the rain had stopped and the sky was clearing. There was light on the horizon. We could move on.

Late that afternoon, Daniel pulled the lead wagon up to the front of the Beaver General Store. While I took Patricia with me into the store to buy supplies, Daniel started off to find the sheriff's office. He wanted to ask where we could safely stop for the night. I shuddered as I thought about last night's experience. We didn't want to repeat it. Under Joe's supervision, the other boys stayed with the wagons. Joe sat up tall as he could, proud to be in charge.

Daniel and I returned at about the same time. Daniel told us all about his conversation with the sheriff, a Mr. Mason.

"He suggested staying at the blacksmiths. We can stay there tonight. There are stables and we can get the horses shoed. We'll be safe here in town. It will also be dry in case it rains again."

"That's a relief," I said. "I hope we can dry things out a bit."

"Did you tell him about the wild man last night?" Joe asked.

"Yes. He wanted to know what the he looked like and what he did. I told him everything."

I interrupted him, "Did you tell him how you had yelled at him and scared him off?"

"I told him I had to chase him off with my rifle. The sheriff thought this man had escaped from a place called

Camp Supply. I guess it's an old Fort turned into an insane asylum. He broke out during the night a couple days ago. They've been out looking for him. Seems he went insane after the War."

The other boys were listening wide-eyed. Joe asked, "How does he know all this?"

"The sheriff got a telegram about him. He's going to let the asylum know we saw him on Beaver Road."

"Will they arrest him?" Joe asked. Daniel shrugged.

I reached over and tousled Joe's brown hair as he grinned at me. "Thanks for staying with the boys and the wagons. You and Daniel are both such great help. Will you and Charlie come in the store to carry out the supplies I bought? Then let's go over to the stables and fix us some supper."

TEN

⚜

Waylaid in Kansas

About Two Weeks Later...

I was close to panic. We had been crossing Kansas on straight roads at right angles, marching across the prairie. Patricia had woken up the day before with a high fever, listless and very hot. She was no better today and I needed to get help, but there were no towns in sight.

When we came upon a rutted path leading over a rise, I told Daniel and Joe to stay with the wagons and to watch their younger brothers. I bundled little Patricia up and rode off on Sally, hoping the path led to a farmhouse. I prayed I would find a friendly family who would respond to my request for help. As the ruts I'd been following dead-ended in a gulch near a wide stream, I saw a small house on the right, smoke curling up from its chimney. Someone was home. As we approached, I thought I saw the curtain at the window move. Maybe this wasn't such a good idea.

I looked down at Patricia. Her head drooped unnaturally to one side and her eyes were glazed with fever.

I took a deep breath. I had to take the risk. I carefully climbed down from Sally and, cradling Patricia and murmuring reassurance to comfort her, I hobbled to the door and knocked.

The door opened a crack and a Negro face with black searching eyes peered out. "Yes, ma'am?"

"My baby daughter's very sick. We're traveling by wagon to Nebraska. I need some help."

The door opened wider to reveal a tidy room with handmade wood furniture. A small woman, with dark brown skin and a kerchief tied around her head, motioned me inside. A fire warmed the room, a cook pot suspended over it from a peg. A colorful pile of quilts was stacked on the sleeping mats near the fireplace. I breathed in the tantalizing odor of fresh bread.

"My name is Sarah Martin. Sorry to disturb you but my baby is very sick. My sons... I left them with our wagons out on the road. Tea...comfrey...do you have some? I'd like to give it to my baby...Then I can leave and travel to the next town."

"Oh, no." The woman shook her head and smiled, revealing a couple of missing teeth. "Ya'll stay right here till she's well. My name's Alida Jones." She reached out to take Patricia from my arms and tenderly laid her on a quilt on a mat on the floor.

"My, she on fire!" she exclaimed. Then she poured cool water from a pitcher on the table into a small bowl, picked up a clean cloth from a shelf under the window, and handed it to me. "Here, cool her down."

I squeezed water over Patricia's feverish little body.

"My boy'll go get your family and bring 'em here," Alida said. "You stay here until this child's better." She went to the door and hollered "Jessy! Come here!"

A dark wiry boy about the same age as Charlie burst through the door. "What do ya want, Ma?" He stopped abruptly, ducked his head and smiled shyly when he saw me. He was bursting with energy, hopping from one foot to the other as he listened to his mother.

"There's wagons out on the road a piece with some boys that belongs to Missus Sarah here. Bring 'em back here." Jessy nodded and started out the door.

"Take my horse, Sally," I said.

Jessy turned, his forehead creased in puzzlement.

"They'll need her to pull one of the wagons. Tell Daniel, he's the oldest, that I said it's all right to bring the children back here. If you tell him my name, Mrs. Sarah Martin, he'll believe you."

A sweet smile filled his face. "Yes'm, I'll tell him."

Alida motioned me to the only chair in the room. "You need to sit and rest. I'll fix some comfrey tea and all of us'll feel better."

When the tea was ready and poured, Alida sat on a stool on the other side of the fire while I rocked Patricia to sleep.

"Did you homestead here?" I asked.

"No, my parents homesteaded here after the Emancipation." Alida responded proudly. "They came up here from Mississippi. It was a long and hard journey but they made it and settled on this land. Where're ya'll from?"

"I grew up in Nebraska where my parents

homesteaded. We lived in a sod house. After I married, my husband and I put in a land claim. Then we moved to Oklahoma and most recently to New Mexico for Sam's health. We had land claims in both places. But my husband died after we were in New Mexico for a year." I paused and swallowed to get rid of the catch in my throat.

Alida murmured her sympathy. "It's hard to lose your man."

I felt compelled to explain the rest of our story to this woman who was a stranger yet seemed so caring and understanding. "I didn't want to stay there... there's no water. So I just left our place there to the rattlesnakes. I'm headed home to Nebraska."

I wondered if Alida was married. "Where's your husband?"

"Oh, George is in town, in Nicodemus. He runs the General Store. His father helped establish the town. George'll be home for supper. And if your baby don't get better, he'll get the doctor in town." Alida spoke with warmth and obvious admiration of her husband.

I was surprised to hear that there was a doctor in such a small town. She went on. "Speaking of supper, I should add some more vegetables to the stew pot. How many children do you have?"

"We can offer some potatoes for the stew and I'm happy to make biscuits." I didn't want to take advantage of her hospitality.

Alida brushed the offer aside. "No need. We have plenty. How many little ones do you have?" she asked again.

"I have four boys and the baby here. My oldest is

sixteen, then fourteen, ten and four. Do you have other children besides Jessy?"

"No. I lost two babies in their first year. I guess there won't be anymore." Alida took a deep breath as if to contain her sadness and then continued. "Jessy is special for us. He does well in school. He goes to a Negro school in Nicodemus with other children from around here. The white children go to the next town over. Tell me about your boys."

Just as I was about to tell her about each of my sons, we heard the wagons and Daniel's voice outside.

I was grateful the boys were on their best behavior as George said grace and we gathered for steaming bowls of stew. Patricia seemed a little less feverish and fell into a sound sleep. After dinner, my boys and Jessy bedded down in the barn. George and Alida's mats were laid out on the other side of the room. As I prepared for the night, Patricia woke up whimpering and very feverish. I spent the night pacing the floor, cradling her, then bathing her in cold water and giving her comfrey tea to drink. At times, she cried out but mostly she was limp and listless. I repeated a constant prayer, asking God to heal her and keep her alive.

As the dawn broke the next morning, I was exhausted from worry and lack of sleep. I had hoped that she would gain strength and recover by this day but my hopes had vanished. She was lifeless when I bathed her again. I splashed her face and tried to wake her up. She was unconscious.

Alida asked George to get the doctor out from town, but George reported that the doctor and his wife had traveled to Dodge City to visit family and wouldn't be back for several days. So Alida spelled me in caring for Patricia while I tried to rest. I was so filled with worry that I would fall asleep and then suddenly jerk wide awake, terrified that Patricia had died while I slept.

Patricia's fever finally broke after two more days and sleepless nights. I am sure the comfrey tea and Alida's loving care helped. Patricia began to giggle and laugh at the boys' rough-housing.

Jessy was studying his spelling words so I decided to have a reading lesson with my boys and include Jessy too. I took out Huckleberry Finn from my wooden box and had each of them read a few pages. Then we talked about the meaning and spelling of the hard words and what the message of the story was. All the boys did well, including Jessy and I loved being the teacher again.

Afterwards, I turned to Alida, "I'd like to ride into Nicodemus to send a telegram to my parents. Since Patricia is getting better, may I leave her with you?" We had been delayed a week now and I knew my father, especially, would be worried when we did not get home as planned.

"Sure, I'd love to watch the baby," Alida assured me.

But when I announced my plans to Daniel, he stiffened, set his jaw and declared, "You can't do that!" I stepped back. He saw the shock on my face. "Those people might hurt you or take advantage of you. You won't be safe. You will get lost." He strung his excuses together, finally announcing, "I won't let you go."

I wondered what had gotten into him. Clearly, I needed to reassure him. "Son, Jessy will ride with me to show me the way."

"But Jessy's just a kid," Daniel protested.

"He knows the way. George runs the General Store. He's a gentleman, as you've seen when he's been home here. I'm sure he's already told the folks in town about us. They're good people and he'll help me get the telegram sent to Grandpa. If your concern is about the Negroes in town it is unfounded."

"Then let me go with you."

"No, I need you to stay here to start packing the wagons. Besides Patricia will be happier if you're around."

"Ma..."

I raised my voice. "I said no. I will go with Jessy and Joe if he wants to come. And that is final."

I turned to speak to Alida and let Daniel deal with his disappointment on his own.

Riding into town, I enjoyed watching Jessy and Joe tease and laugh together. I was so pleased that all the boys were getting along so well with Jessy. It was good for them to have some companionship.

The ride into town was smooth and easy and I let my mind wander back over our journey so far. We had survived the challenges and I was grateful that I hadn't lost Daniel to the quicksand or Patricia to the fever. I couldn't bear another loss.

I'd been so vulnerable since Sam died. I resented that he left me in that Godforsaken place with a six-month-old infant. How did I manage? But I reminded myself that I'd spent several winters without Sam, alone with the children. I could handle this trip. And Daniel was such a help, but this last exchange surprised me. He could be so stubborn, just like his father! I wondered if he was afraid of the Negroes in town. This was his first real experience being close to them. After all, I'd had experience with the Negroes when we first moved to Nebraska. They worked around the rail yard and I went with my older brother to take them a roasting hen or some eggs when they didn't have enough to eat and their wages were delayed.

I was lost in thought when I heard Joe hollering at me. "Look, Ma!" I looked up as we turned onto the dusty main street to see the sign, "George's General Store" painted in large block letters above the door. The building was unpainted rough boards but appeared to be well built, better than the other buildings, which looked rather crudely thrown together. Across the street stood the only two-story building, a rooming house, and café. In the center of town there was a small whitewashed church, its steeple pointing up to the blue sky.

Then I saw what the boys were yelling about. It was one of those new-fangled automobiles out front of the General Store. The boys jumped down from their mounts and ran around it excitedly. Sam had told me about seeing automobiles in Phoenix when he was there, but no one we knew had one. I wondered who owned this one.

When we walked into the store, George was chatting with a well-dressed Negro couple. I could hear comments about an event at the school house. It sounded like they were concerned about what had happened. But as George caught sight of me and the two boys, he stopped mid-sentence, broke into a smile and rushed over to grab my arm and guide me to a chair. His booming voice filled the store as he introduced Joe and me to Dr. and Mrs. Royce. "This is the nice widow taking her family to Nebraska that's staying with us," he explained.

"Dr. Royce just bought the Model T you saw out front, down in Dodge City!" he added, turning to me. "Pretty exciting isn't it?"

"How exciting! I've never seen one... Just heard about them."

"We bought it used. It will help me get to my patients," Dr. Royce said. "I understand you could have used my services a few days ago. I am sorry I wasn't available."

"Thank you. Yes, my baby daughter had a very high fever but she's fine now. We'll be leaving soon for Nebraska." I turned to smile at Mrs. Royce.

She asked, "Where are you traveling from?"

"New Mexico," I answered.

"What a long journey you're making," she said. "Especially for someone who's not well."

"George and Alida generously gave us a place to stay. I am very grateful." I turned to George. "I want to send a telegram to my father to let him know we've been delayed, but that we're all fine."

"You write it out and I'll send it," George said.

When we returned from town, Joe and Jessy told Daniel, Charlie and Alida about the Model T automobile.

"Much easier travel than our wagons," I joked with Alida. "We must get back on the road." If we washed clothes and finished packing the wagons tomorrow, when the clothes dried, we could head out. My eyes began to tear up. "Alida, I'm so grateful for your hospitality. How can I ever repay you?"

I felt Alida's warm embrace as her soothing voice reassured me. "Sarah, my dear, you've more than repaid me with the love and gentleness you brought into our home, your kindness to me and your help with Jessy's school work. We'll miss you and the children."

The next day was bustling as we got ready to move on. Daniel and I heated water to do the wash, hung it up to dry and packed the rest of our belongings into the wagon. Daniel was outside arranging the supplies we had purchased in town when I heard a horse galloping toward the house.

"Where's your mother?" George asked Daniel, his loud voice carrying inside. "I have something for her."

"She's inside." I heard Daniel reply. The door slammed shut and George rushed in.

"George, whatever is the hurry?" I asked. "We aren't leaving for two more days. Here, sit down for a minute."

Taking a deep breath, George handed me a telegram and stepped back without a word. I ripped it open and scanned it quickly. "No!" Everything swirled around me. I heard Patricia crying, felt an arm around my shoulders comforting me. There were voices asking, wondering, bewildered. Someone took the telegram from me.

Then I heard Daniel's voice. "My grandfather died yesterday," he said.

ELEVEN

❧

Nebraska Welcomes Us Home

One Week Later...

The trip across the rest of the Kansas prairie was without incident. Some of the land had been homesteaded and was cultivated with acres of corn and wheat lining the straight dirt roads. Other areas were dry prairie for long distances, the road wandering and curving around hills. In some of the draws and gullies, cattle grazed. Since we'd left George and Alida, I'd sat at the front of the wagon staring at nothing. My mind was empty. When I got so tired that I couldn't hold myself up, Daniel helped me climb into the wagon to rest. When I closed my eyes, I could see my father smiling at me, welcoming us home. But when I reached out toward him, he would vanish and only the empty prairie remained.

Fortunately, the boys made few demands, knowing that I couldn't help with much of anything. Only Patricia, who was too young to understand, demanded attention. When we stopped for the night, I did only what was necessary to get the children fed. Daniel was the helpful son but I suspected that he felt ignored.

One evening, we set up camp near the Platte River, a few days after we'd crossed into Nebraska. After supper, Joe spoke up. "Ma, tell me more about Grandpa. I don't remember him very well."

I was surprised to discover a sense of relief at the idea of telling stories about my adored father.

"Papa was a proud man with a strong pioneer spirit," I began. "He saw his responsibility to care and provide for his family as his most important accomplishment. When they were newly married, he walked with his new wife, my mother and your Grandma, with all of their worldly possessions in a one-horse cart from Indiana to Iowa in search of the right land. He wanted a place to raise a family that had water and timber. Very different from our land in New Mexico."

Charlie interrupted, "Did he find it? Water, I mean?"

"Oh yes!" I laughed for the first time in days. "In Iowa, where Mama and Papa settled, we had a well with plenty of water. The land was green and lush with lots of rivers, streams and rain."

"Did they follow a road from Indiana that took them to Iowa?" Joe's question seemed to be on the minds of the other boys too, since they nodded and leaned forward, eager to hear more.

"We have roads to follow now. But, imagine what it would be like to follow rough trails through heavily wooded forests and across many rivers and streams. They walked the whole way beside the wagon. And, like you boys are doing, they slept on the ground at night.

"When they found the right place in Iowa, they filed a land claim and settled down to farming and raising a family. Papa was protective of all of us, especially the girls, yet he expected each of us to carry our share of the work on the farm. We all had chores to do as soon as we were three or four years old. Just like your father and I have expected each of you to share the work."

"Yeah, we all do our chores. Except Petey doesn't have to do much... or Patricia," Charlie said. "Patricia's too little, but when will Petey have to do his share? He's already four."

"I help," Petey said.

Daniel gave Petey an affectionate pat. "You'll do more when you're strong enough that we don't worry about you, right, Ma?"

"I think Petey's helped a lot on this trip, haven't you, son? You've carried things to help load the wagon. I'm sure you'll be strong enough for chores when we get to Nebraska." Petey nodded vigorously and grinned.

"I remember my first chore," I went on. "It was when I was about three or four and I had to find the eggs the chickens laid around the barn while my older sister followed me with the bucket. When I became strong enough to carry the bucket, my younger sister searched for the eggs. My older brothers had to feed the livestock, milk the cows and help with the planting. At different times, we all had to gather fruit and vegetables from Mama's garden.

"You boys know how important I think going to school and getting an education is. Both your grandparents believed the same thing. In fact, Papa thought it was so important that he donated the land across the road from our house for the school house. Like all of you, we were expected to go to school. But we didn't have to ride very far, we just walked across the road. Sometimes Papa hitched up the sleigh to take other kids home from school when a blizzard blew in. For him, the weather was never an excuse to stay home from school."

"You taught us when we stayed home because of the weather," Joe said. "Did your Ma help you with your lessons?"

"Not much. She couldn't read or write very well. I think that's why she and Papa placed so much emphasis on all of us kids completing school. They wouldn't let my older brothers leave school until they were at least sixteen, even though other boys often left at twelve or thirteen. Two of my older sisters became teachers like I did."

"Ma, I'm going to find work when we get to Nebraska, maybe work on a farm," Daniel said. "I want to work. I don't want to go to school anymore." I started to object, but he went on. "I'm sixteen. I'm a man now. I can help support you."

"You're right, son. You've proven yourself as a man on this trip. I'm proud of you. I'll be grateful for your help.

"I know you're getting sleepy and soon it will be time for bed," I said, addressing all of my children. "But, I have one more story about Papa. It's also about history here in the United States. Papa had strong beliefs about the value of human life and refused to point a gun at another human being. Since he was older and already had a family when the Civil War started, he chose another way to support the Union cause. Do you remember learning about the Civil War?"

"It was the war to free the slaves and save the Union," Joe said.

"Papa was adamantly opposed to slavery and believed in the cause of freeing the slaves. So, he left his farm in Iowa with his team and wagon and went to the Mississippi River to haul Union troops to the boat landings."

"Ma, what is slavery?"Charlie asked. "I don't understand."

"We have very sad history in the United States of buying and selling other human beings," I explained. "Negroes were captured against their will and brought here from Africa a long time ago. They were sold to land owners as slaves. As slaves, they were not free to do what they wanted, only what their owners wanted. Many were brutally beaten and treated badly.

"We fought the Civil War because there was a big disagreement about slavery. Some people believed it was acceptable to own another human being and they thought Negroes were not very smart. They were willing to fight for the right to own slaves and believed in that right so strongly they were willing to break away from the United States and form another country. They were called Confederates.

"People on the other side of the argument, the Union side, wanted to keep the country together and wanted to free the slaves because they believed slavery was wrong. My father believed that, too."

"Do you believe it was wrong?" Charlie asked.

"Yes, I do. Because of the strong feelings on both

sides, we fought a bitter war which divided our country. Your father fought with the Union long before I met him."

"Did he win?" Charlie asked.

Daniel spoke up. "You ninny! It's not whether a person won. It's whether the Union side beat the Confederate side!"

"So, who won?" Charlie demanded.

"The Union, of course," Daniel said. "I learned in school that one of the important generals in the Civil War, General Sherman, supposedly said that the United States should declare war on Mexico and force them to take back New Mexico. I guess he didn't like the dry land in New Mexico and thought it was useless." We all laughed, remembering our own experience with the lack of water.

"Ma, were George and Alida slaves?" Daniel ventured.

"No, but their parents were. They lived in a state in the South called Mississippi. After the war ended, when they learned they had been freed by President Lincoln, they headed North. They escaped a very brutal master. They walked carrying their meager belongings all the way to Kansas."

"Why Kansas?" Daniel asked.

"Because they heard they could settle there and own their own farm. George and Alida live on the land that her parents settled. George's parents started the town with a General Store."

"Where did all the other ones come from?" Joe spoke up for the first time since he asked about Grandpa.

"You mean the other Negroes that live in Nicodemus? Probably from Mississippi and other states in the South. I imagine their stories are similar. They, too, wanted freedom, a new life, land to farm and a chance to raise their families. Negroes want the same things that we all do"

Daniel was squirming around a bit. I guessed he might be feeling a little uncomfortable about his earlier judgments. I hoped that his suspicions about the Negroes in the town of Nicodemus had been reduced now.

After a few quiet moments, he said, "I'd like to hear more about Grandpa and what he thought about the Negroes."

"Grandpa had strong beliefs that no human being should be owned by another. He believed it was important to give the Negroes a chance to be educated and learn a trade because most of them had been denied an education as slaves. I heard him talk about this as I grew up. When I was fifteen we moved from Iowa to Nebraska because my older brother Fred was laying the railroad track there. There were some Negroes that did some of the hard labor at the rail yard. We used to bring food to them when they didn't have enough to eat.

"Papa and Mama helped lots of people in the community in Thomas County. They were respected and well liked. In fact, they elected Papa as the Justice of the Peace and then a County Judge because of his reputation for honesty and fair dealing."

I felt tears of pride mixed with sadness well up. "Your Grandpa was a good man. He taught me a lot. I will miss him." As the tears spilled over, I knew Papa would be proud of me and how I had managed to bring my children from New Mexico to Nebraska. With that recognition, I sat up straight, lifted my head and smiled through my tears with the memories of his love and support. I looked around at my boys. They were quiet. Petey had fallen asleep with his head on Daniel's knee. The others were pensive. I felt strong, supported by my father's love and more confident than I had during our whole trip.

Ten Days Later...

Daniel turned the wagon into the yard of the family homestead. We were finally home! It had taken us over two months to get here. Breathless, I watched for the stand of cottonwood trees which shaded and protected the sod house that had been my parent's home for so many years. Papa had never gotten around to building a big fancy house for Mama as he had promised when they first homesteaded this land. She had always brushed it off, saying she wouldn't know what to do with a bigger house. I wondered what she would do now—maybe move into town or move in with one of my brothers.

It looked like the whole family was waiting for us. Nieces and nephews were jumping up and down. I could see my older brother Robert and his wife, Millie, my younger brother Andrew and Jane, my older sister, Bernice and her husband Phil. I was so happy to see them all. But most of all, I was thrilled to see Mama who stood behind the others with a smile that lit up her face. As we pulled up, Bernice reached for Patricia who smiled and went to her willingly. Robert helped me down from the wagon. His brown eyes crinkled at the corners, his smile as broad as the Platte River.

"My favorite little sister's home again!" he exclaimed.

With tears in my eyes, I hugged Mama. "I'm so happy to see you and so sad that Papa isn't here." Her arms tightened around me.

"Uncle Robert," Daniel said, "can we pull the team and the mules into the barn?"

"Of course. Paul'll help you, won't you, Paul?" Robert turned to a boy of twelve who was a young image of my brother Andrew.

Daniel and Joe jumped up onto the wagons and turned the horses and mules toward the large well-built two-story structure behind the house. "Wow," I heard Daniel with a loud whisper to Joe. "That barn's nicer than most of the houses in New Mexico. I wonder what the second floor's for."

Charlie fell in beside Paul grinning and bouncing around. I thought he must be secretly relieved that Petey was no longer his only choice for companionship.

That evening over a delicious supper, I basked in the welcoming warmth from my family as the children and I told stories of our trip—the thief who tried to take our sack of flour, the talented horse Ezekiel who helped us ford the river and save Daniel from the quicksand, the crazy man who tried to get up on Socks, and the warm hospitality of George and Alida.

After dinner, I sat with Robert and Millie in front of the fire. Andrew and Jane had taken Mama back to her house. My children and the rest of the family had all found their way to bed.

Millie looked at me with her compassionate brown eyes and said, "Sarah, how are you managing? I know you must be sad losing Sam, but you seem stronger and more independent than when you left Nebraska so many years ago."

"There are times when I am lonely and sad." I couldn't tell her that I resented that Sam left me alone with five children. "I was counting on Papa for some reassurance and support. I took his death very hard." I paused to take a breath and keep the tears from taking over my words.

Millie nodded. "You were very close to him."

The tears cascaded down my face for a few minutes. When I finally stopped crying, I plunged ahead. "I do miss Sam's quiet strength, his ability to sort through things and make decisions. I miss his sense of humor. Of course, I knew I'd be alone eventually given the difference in our ages."

"How much older was he?" Robert asked.

"Thirty years. I always knew he'd die before me, but I wasn't prepared for the burden of being responsible for raising the children alone. I do feel stronger now and better able to cope than I did a few months ago. Each challenge we met on this trip, I grew more confident in my ability to manage without Sam. But it isn't over yet."

"Did he leave you anything? How will you support yourself and your children?" Robert was always direct. He went on before I could answer. "And did you ever find out what all he did before you met? Maybe he has land somewhere that you can sell. He did say he worked cattle."

I shook my head. "That's unlikely. I only know a few stories of his earlier life. It was a hard rough life. I'm sure he didn't have any land or money hidden away. I'm going to file a land claim here and I hope to get Widow's Benefits since he was a Civil War veteran. I've already filed the papers."

"Good. Maybe it won't be too long 'fore you get your money. I hope nothing gets in the way." With that Robert got up and said, "Good night. You know we're here for you."

"Thank you," I said.

Millie got up and gave me a hug. "Sarah, dear, you can stay with us as long as you need while you get settled and get your benefits."

PART 2: WILL

FORT WORTH, TEXAS

1878

TWELVE

The Opportunity to Escape

The hay was tickling his nose but Will didn't dare sneeze or even move. The voices and footsteps were coming toward the stables. He held his breath and wished his pounding heart wasn't so loud. His throat was dry, his body tense.

"I thought I saw him run this way." The voice sounded tentative.

A second voice responded, chuckling, "Didn't expect a hay shoveler to be that fast with a gun."

"Well, no-one's going to miss Graham too much, not even his wife. He was a mean SOB." The first voice spoke again.

A third voice added, "Yeah, that's true but that sod buster did kill him. Maybe he's not really a sodbuster. Bein' a Texas Ranger, I...

"Hey, looking for someone?" Will had heard that voice before. He tried to place it.

"Yeah, mister," the third voice answered, "we're looking for a sod buster in overalls and a vest. Bushwacked a man in the saloon. Have you seen him?"

Will's breath caught in his throat. Did this guy see

him dive into the hay? Who was he anyway? Would he turn him in? He listened intently.

"Who are ya anyway?" the first voice demanded. "Were ya in the saloon? Did ya see the hay shoveler kill–"

"Hold it, Macon. Don't ask so many questions? Give the guy a chance to talk."

The familiar voice spoke again. "I'm a trail boss. Getting' ready to drive a herd of longhorns up the trail to Dodge City. And yeah, I saw the sod buster who killed the drunk in the saloon. He asked for it."

Will relaxed a bit. Now he knew that this guy was the cowboy who bought him a whiskey at the bar before he went over to play at the card table. He'd offered him a job on the trail crew.

"That's beside the point," one of the other voices responded. "Need to find the killer and arrest him."

Will's stomach clenched. Fear rose like sour food from his stomach into his throat. What was he going to do to get out of this? Where could he go?

The trail boss spoke up again, "Well ya'd better get on your mounts and go after him, then. He's headed out on his mount going south and galloping fast."

After the men cleared out, Will lay in the quiet of the stables listening and wondering. He was angry with himself for getting into this mess. He pictured the card player he'd shot. He was a Reb, a Gray Back, one of those proud Texans who refer to the War of Northern Aggression with resentment. Will shuddered as he remembered how drunk the man was. He had called Will a "Billy Yank" and curled his lip, taunting Will about drinkin' the cheap whiskey he called "tonsil varnish."

What was he going to do? These Rangers were after him. Could he get out of town? Should he leave now and go back home? Why did the trail boss lie for him?

He thought back to the card game in the tavern again. He had been sitting across the table from a drunk arrogant loser. He saw a flash of silver as the man pulled his gun from his belt. He'd felt a bullet whizz past his ear, then he ducked behind a table and fired. Chairs hit the floor as men scrambled out of the way. "Why did I fire again?" Will asked himself." That's when he groaned. "The second shot killed him."

He thought about Delia, pregnant with their sixth child. She was going to deliver soon. He needed to get feed corn back to their farm for the hogs. They were going to deliver soon, too. He needed to get home. Maybe he could get to his wagon and team and get out of town now. It was the middle of the night. He would be going west and, thanks to the trail boss, they would look for him going south.

Now, here in the stable, it was quiet and dark. He needed to escape. He gingerly climbed out of the hay and came face to face with the trail boss, sitting on a hay bale.

"Hey, buster, where are ya goin'? Think ya're going to sneak out of here without getting caught by those Texas Rangers? Ha!"

"Why did you lie for me? What's in it for you?" Will asked.

"I watched that guy goad other cowboys at the table. He asked for it. He's an SOB. Besides, I thought maybe I could interest ya now in joining my crew. I'll cover for ya and we can get out of town by day after tomorrow."

"But I have a wife and kids. They're expecting me back home in three weeks. And I've never driven cattle before."

"We'll be gone four or five weeks. This will simmer down by then. Better to go home late than not go home at all."

Will considered what the man had said. Delia would be angry. She hadn't wanted him to leave at all. She'd begged him to stay home, the baby would come soon. But they needed the corn for the hogs. Now, he might not get home at all. What if he was caught and they strung him up? "Mister, do ya need a cook?" he asked. "I cooked for some of the wagon trains coming west after the war."

"Cookie, it's a deal," the trail boss answered. "Name's Jake. Go get yourself some cowboy clothes so ya don't look like a hayseed. Lay low and we'll head out day after tomorrow. Meet here at the stables."

That morning, Will snuck off to the barber to shave off his mustache and have his hair cut short. He ditched his overalls and vest, bought a new hat, shirt and Levi's. Now he looked like a cowboy. Jake had told him they were moving cattle up to Fort Dodge. The drive would take at least four weeks, probably more. By then, Will thought, the Rangers would be looking for the latest killer and he could escape. He could buy some corn and head home. He was still worried about Delia and the children. She'd be as cross as a snapping turtle, but at least he'd have a little extra and he could buy her something pretty to wear after the baby was born.

THIRTEEN

The Cattle Drive

At first light on the second day out, Will was serving breakfast. He took a big swig of coffee and rang the chow bell. Cooking for hungry cowboys wasn't too bad. They demanded to be fed, but they didn't need anything fancy. Breakfast was bacon, coffee and biscuits or what the men called "sinkers." As they ate, Will looked around at the men. Some of them were pretty young, not much older than his son, Willy. They were looking for excitement, happy to walk around with their irons and brag about their exploits. The older ones were there for the money. "We just want an easy drive north," they said. He shared their sentiment.

He enjoyed the camaraderie of this crew. It reminded him of his time in the Union Army–sleeping on the ground, boring food, dirty, no women or home comforts. A hard life. But it was eased by the easy-going company of men joking with each other, telling stories or singing around the campfire. Being here was like putting on old boots that had molded to your feet. He didn't need to worry about these men learning his secret. Cowboys minded their own business. He was sure their pasts weren't pure and no one asked any questions, including Jake.

This morning the wranglers were identifying their mounts for the day from the remuda, the herd of horses brought along to provide a fresh pony on the long ride. Will was packing up the chuck box when he heard one of the wranglers yelling at Jake. "Looks like we got company comin'." He pointed toward the dust cloud kicked up by half dozen riders coming up behind the cattle on the west.

After yelling, "Keep on!" to the crew, Jake rode out to meet the riders, who were now riding up near the edge of the herd. Will pulled his hat down and busied himself loading up the Dutch oven, coffee pot, plates and cups into the chuck box and the drovers' bedrolls into the wagon. He positioned himself so he could watch without being too obvious. When he caught the glint of a badge on one of the men riding up, the thumping in his chest got louder. These riders were Texas Rangers and they were after him.

Jake's voice carried in the early morning air above the low noises of the cattle. His greeting was friendly, like he knew them. "No, we haven't seen any signs of a lone rider," Jake said. "Haven't seen anyone." One of the Rangers asked more questions. Jake answered, "No need to talk to the crew. We haven't seen signs of anyone out here." After more comments from the Rangers, Jake said, "Sure, I'll watch for him and let ya know if we see anyone. Good luck!" Then he rode back to the herd and the waiting wranglers. "Move out!" he called.

Will relaxed, took a deep breath and wondered why Jake had saved his life again. He cracked the whip over the oxen pulling the chuck wagon to move out.

Several Days Later...

That morning, Will noticed a young wrangler approached Jake. "Hey Boss, I wanna move from drag to flank. Too hard. Too much dust. I can do flank now." The drag rider had the dirtiest, dustiest job on the drive, following the herd and rounding up stragglers. "Ya're not ready yet to ride flank," Jake responded. "Ya'll need to stay on drag." The kid kept pushing. "I don't wanna ride drag. Someone else can do it." He started yelling. "How do ya know I'm not ready? I'm as ready as anyone else!"

Will remembered his own adolescent arrogance when he demanded that Uncle Bill pay him the same as the experienced adult men who worked on the farm back in Indiana. And his rudeness when he cussed out the Sargent in his army unit, who expected them to head out at midnight without a decent meal and no sleep. He'd been cocky and overconfident then, too inexperienced to realize they would be ambushed by the Confederate troops if they didn't make tracks and get the hell out of that river valley. He could have been charged with insubordination, but the Sargent was anxious to get the men out. Looking back, he realized he'd just been trying to prove himself.

This kid probably wanted to prove himself too. He didn't realize that pushing wouldn't get him anywhere. Jake just kept repeating in an even voice, "Sorry, kid, I can't do that." But the kid was touchy as a teased snake. When he threatened to quit if he didn't get whatever he was asking, Jake replied calmly, "You think about it. Let me know by the end of the day." That kid was still smokin' when he came to get his pay. Jake, in contrast, had stayed calm as a quiet pond on a lazy summer afternoon. By sunset, the kid was high-balling it out of camp.

That night the air was heavy and hot, black as a cast iron pot. Tom, the lead rider, joked, "It's so dark the drovers can't find their noses with both hands." The animals were restless and milled around, bawling, knowing instinctively that something was about to happen. It was a lot different tonight than the other nights on the trail when the animals bedded down and the drovers all served a turn, two at a time, as night guards for a couple of hours. They would circle the bed ground of the cattle in opposite directions to ensure no animals slipped away during the night.

Tonight, Jake, ordered all the drovers onto their mounts to ride among the herd. They were sweating anxiously like the nervous critters they hoped to control. They wore metal all over their bodies—gun, spurs, knife, canteen—all deadly attractions for bolts of stray lightning. Over the sound of the herd, the high clear tenor voice of Pedro, the Mexican cowboy crooned, "Home, home on the range, where the deer and the antelope play..." His voice was soothing to the longhorns, just as it helped the crew forget their troubles when he sang at night around the campfire after a hard day on the trail. Pedro was risking his life riding among cattle that could stampede at any moment. Will admired his courage as he listened to Pedro's melodious voice soar.

As the dough wrangler, known by everyone as "Cookie", he didn't normally ride the herd. His job was to provide the grub for these hardworking "waddies" as Jake referred to the crew. But this night Jake had hollered for "all hands and the cook." It was an emergency and he also needed an extra hand, because that young cowboy had gotten his bristles up and quit. Managing the crew on these drives to Fort Dodge was a challenge many men on the frontier didn't want or couldn't do. Will couldn't imagine leading a crew, dealing with smart-ass kids and old hands who knew too much. Jake seemed well suited, though. He had the respect of the men and remained unruffled, even in a crisis. And tonight, with a storm imminent and the herd on edge, was no exception.

Will had learned from Tom, the lead point rider on the crew, how these Texas longhorns were different from other domestic cattle. Their ancestry came mostly from Spanish cattle brought north as early as 1690, mixed with some blood from Anglo-American cattle. The longhorn was a powerful animal with long legs, hard hoofs and an ability to survive long treks with minimal grass and water, which suited them to trail life. However, they were haughty animals, skittish and always on the defensive, and those horns extended three to eight feet from tip to tip.

Will was nervous as he thought about Tom's warning that these animals would accept a cowboy riding among them on a horse, but if the rider was knocked off or the horse stumbled and fell, the longhorn would challenge anything that moved near the earth. A drover's life was at risk. A stampede could begin from anything that startled the herd—a flash of lightning, the bang of a cup, or even the flare of a match. Will had heard the old hands tell stories about dangerous stampedes. Now he felt the trickle of sweat become a river running down his back and realized he was clutching the reins far too tightly. His stiff finger, injured in the war was aching.

He wanted to be home doing routine chores like feeding the hogs, putting up fence posts or having supper with Delia and the kids and eating biscuits to sop up the broth from rabbit stew. His guts cramped as he waited for the storm and a potential stampede. Electricity was in the air. Will was amazed as he watched the phosphorescence that danced between the horns of the steers and around the cowboys' hats. He watched it jump from the horns of one animal to the next. No wonder they were restless. In the far distance, the sky lit up. The storm was moving fast. Jake motioned to pull in the circumference of cattle to keep them closer together.

For a moment, the sky was suddenly as bright as daylight and the boom that followed shook the ground. On the far side of the herd from Will, the cattle took off. Jake, Tom and the other point rider spurred their horses off to the left, leaning low over their saddles, riding like the devil was after them. Will thought how they must be praying that their horses would avoid the prairie dog holes. It was pitch black and the rain was suddenly coming down in torrents. Despite this, the cowboys managed to get their horses abreast of the lead steers.

Will knew from the stories the drovers told that Tom as the lead point rider would spur his horse ahead of the lead steer and with the other point rider they would try to change the animals' direction. Other lead steers would likely try to keep going straight ahead but between the two point riders galloping ahead they would get them all turned to the right. Then with the help of the other cowboys, the rest of the herd would follow. The lead steers would begin slowing down. Soon the entire herd would be going in a circle. Finally, the cattle, exhausted from running, would be controlled.

Jake wheeled up sharply on his horse next to Will. When the lightening flashed, Will caught a deep line of worry across his face. "Have ya seen Tom?" Jake asked. "He's missing." Will shook his head no and Jake galloped off. Will had stayed at the back of the herd near the chuck wagon while the cowboys raced to contain the frightened cattle. Now, he spurred his mount and rode to the edges of the milling cattle, searching.

Tom was the most experienced and best hand that Jake had. He had the honored post as the point rider with the greatest responsibility. He and Jake had ridden many drives together and were good friends. Tom joked they were close enough to use the same toothpick. The three of them often exchanged stories of serving in the army, cooking on the frontier, working cattle, and driving wagon trains. Will was more comfortable around the two of them than the rest of the crew. Most were friendly enough except for two tough-looking hombres who split off by themselves most nights. They seemed almost hostile and they didn't joke or tell stories with the rest of the crew.

The thunder and lightning had stopped, helping to keep the cattle calm. But now it was as dark as midnight under a skillet. Will could only see a foot or two in front of his horse. The rain ran off his hat and clothes and into his boots. He was shaking from the chill of his damp clothes—or was it from his fear of finding Tom trampled to a gruesome death?

FOURTEEN

Crossing the Red River

A Week Later

The crew sat around the campfire. The older cowboys told tales about river crossings to scare the young ones. Will thought they were succeeding, but he knew the bravado in the stories cloaked their own fear. The rain had been a steady downpour for two days, a real gully washer, as Tom said. Yesterday the Red River, a shade of muddy clay, was lapping over its banks. The fast-flowing current carried logs and branches which occasionally caught on trees and boulders where the water lapped at the river's edge. Eventually, the power of the water tore loose the growing collection of logs and branches, which would once again swing into the swirl of the rushing water.

The prospect of swimming the herd across this flood stage river was giving everyone the jitters. To damp their nervousness, the men passed around the bag of Bull Durham, rolling cigarettes, pacing back and forth, telling flood stories, each one more unbelievable than the last. Despite the jumpiness of his crew, Jake leaned back against a rock just as calm as a toad sitting in the sun. Will wondered if his guts would be churning when they led those ornery longhorns into the river. And he wondered how Tom would manage with his injuries.

Will had patched up Tom the night of the stampede. Turned out, after the herd was beginning to quiet down, lightning struck nearby and stunned Tom's horse, felling them both. He was lucky that his horse scrambled up with him on it and lucky not to get trampled. But, unfortunately, one of those half-ton doggies did step on his foot. Will had cut off his boot and wrapped his swollen foot and ankle. Since then, Tom had continued riding with his mangled foot. But could he manage to get these animals across the river?

Will and Tom had become closer during the course of the drive and Tom began to confide in Will some of his own storied past. Will was tempted to let Tom know he was on the dodge from the law. But he caught himself and kept his secret.

Will hadn't realized until the morning's discussion at breakfast after the storm that five head of cattle had been lost from the first bolt of lightning that struck right in the midst of the herd. Losing cattle was costly.

"I was hoping to get about $2.95 per 100 pounds," Jake had told Will "Almost three times what they bring in Texas–only about ten bucks a head."

Now, with so much rain, there was the potential of losing more cattle crossing the swollen river.

They'd taken the Cimarron Cut-Off at the Red Fork Ranch where the boys enjoyed some rest, whiskey and cards. Will didn't play, although he was tempted. He had been playing since he was a kid having learned from his Uncle Bill, the riverboat captain who would teach him new tricks each time he returned from New Orleans. Will had gotten pretty good and won some serious money during his stint in the army. Although, he hadn't played much since he settled down with Delia. She didn't approve. He was confident he could beat these cowboys. But, he didn't want to take a risk. He was afraid his luck would run muddy like the Red River.

The next day, they were at the River waiting for the crest to fall. They began getting ready to cross after Jake decided they would swim the herd tomorrow. First, he wanted to float the chuck wagon across. The wagon oxen would lead the rest of the herd into the swirling water.

The next day the wranglers drove the lead steer into the river following the oxen and the cook wagon. Longhorns don't like water. Some of the orneriest animals kept trying to turn around. But the drovers herded, led, and cajoled them into the river, swimming against the current behind the lead steers. Tom and two other drovers intercepted three cattle who almost succeeded in getting up the bank. But, they spurred their horses and drove them back into the river.

When Will got the oxen and the wagon to the other side, the oxen struggled up the embankment, slipping back into the river. After a couple of tries, they reached flat ground. After Will tied them up, he looked back. Few sights could compare to the hundreds of horns and noses sticking out of the water coming right at you, he thought.

Those drovers were damned skilled; they hadn't lost a single head.

Then he saw Tom flailing downstream. "Where are the other drovers? Don't they see Tom?" he muttered. But, they were working the cattle, yelling, corralling and urging them across the dangerous current. No one was paying attention to Tom and his cries did not carry over the rushing river and the bawling animals.

Will jumped on his horse, galloped along the banks downstream, past the herd and plunged into the raging river. His horse struggled against the current, which threatened to carry them further down the river. "I might be the cook, but right now I need to be a cowboy," he said to himself as he readied his rope to throw to Tom. Throwing a rope was not a cowboy skill he had ever learned. But Tom wasn't looking, instead, he disappeared under the water. When he came back up, he thrashed about, his eyes wide with panic, his arms waving wildly. Finally, he caught sight of Will.

Will hurriedly flung the rope towards him, but he missed and Tom went under again. As Will scanned the water, it seemed like a long time before his head appeared further downstream. Will urged his horse closer to Tom. He took a deep breath hoping to calm his own panic. "Steady," he muttered to himself. He twirled the rope and aimed more carefully this time. "Whew," Will let out a breath of relief as Tom caught the rope and positioned it under his arms. Will spurred his horse up onto the bank, then moved slowly backward, pulling Tom out.

That night around the campfire, as he sat with his

injured leg propped up on a log, a grateful Tom thanked Will. "Ya dumb cowpokes would have let me drown, but Will here risked riding down the river in that current, and pulled me out! Cookie, ya'll do to ride the river with! I owe ya twice now."

Jake grinned, clearly approving the risk Will had taken. The rest of the crew joked about riding the river with a dough wrangle, all in good humor, except for the two men who kept themselves apart. Instead, one curled his lip and said with a sneer, "Flour flusher! Ya aren't a real dough wrangler. I'd never choose to ride the river with ya!"

Later that night, Will lay on his bedroll looking up at the stars and listening to the sounds of the night—the river rushing by, the crack of the embers in the dying campfire, the low rustling of the cattle, the snoring of the cowboys. He found himself wondering about those two bitter and angry wranglers. Better to stay out of their way.

FIFTEEN

Oklahoma

*O*nce across the Red River, they were in Oklahoma.
After what seemed like weeks of traveling across empty
plains, they passed a hand-scrawled sign next to the trail,
saying "1 Wohaw."

"It means the Indians expect one steer in exchange
for grazing privileges," said Tom in answer to Will's questioning look.

"So what will they do if they don't get it?" Will asked.

"Cause trouble. Jake will give them a steer to prevent it."

"Do other trail bosses give in to them, too?"

"It's not giving in. It's preventing trouble. Other trail
bosses who don't provide the steer have their herds stam-
peded in the night. That usually means losing more than
one."

They hadn't gotten far beyond the river when one of
the crew yelled and pointed off to the west. Will turned
to see about fifty braves on Indian ponies on the crest of
the hill. He checked his holster and gun, and then stopped
to watch as two braves rode toward Jake. He waved and

offered a friendly greeting.

Will was surprised to see Jake sitting casually on his horse as the braves rode toward him. A smile played around his mouth and his brows lifted in anticipation. Will looked toward Tom, who had ridden over to join Jake. They seemed to ride silently to meet the braves. Then the braves held up three fingers and shouted "Wohaw."

"No, one wohaw," Jake responded, holding up a forefinger. Will felt the sweat trickle down his back. Two more braves rode up to join the negotiation.

Will wasn't the only one who was nervous. He noticed the rest of the drovers hung back. They kept adjusting their holsters and sat unusually straight in the saddles. Their faces taut, their foreheads shiny with sweat. Would the braves attack? Will sucked in his breath. Then he noticed those same two wranglers who'd sneered at him at the Red River, watching him. Their eyes narrowed and they scowled at him. A shiver went up his back. I need to stay away from those two characters, he thought and turned back to watch Jake's negotiations with the Indians again.

After some discussion, Tom broke away from the group and cut out two steers, moving them toward the braves. Will guessed that Jake had decided that peace with the Indians was worth the cost of the second steer. Hopefully, the drive could continue across Indian Territory without worry.

Will paused on a rise looking over the vast sunbaked prairie, impressed by the line of cattle that stretched out in front of him. Jake had slowed the herd so that they could get water along the bank at the river. Here were the endless grasslands Will had heard about, spreading in all directions as far as the eye could see. And it was hot, hot enough to wither a fence post. No man or beast should move in this heat. But at least it was better than the drought or the grasshopper plagues he'd heard about. The grass was good this year, high and green. He thought of his two youngest children laughing and running hand-in-hand across the prairie. Then he imagined his oldest son sitting on a horse, a pace ahead, waiting for him. Will realized he wanted to go home. But as soon as he did, the guilt rose up sour in his gut. Would Delia take him back?

The horizon shimmered invitingly in the distance, like a lake with the sun bouncing off the ripples. But it was a mirage and the cattle knew it as well as he did. They were headed for the wide river bed to quench their thirst and lie in the mud to cool off before they had to continue on in this unbearable heat.

Will let the oxen find their own way down the embankment to the stream. They could smell the water and, though they were clearly thirsty, they avoided the prairie dog holes and hidden boulders on the way down. After Will found a level spot for the wagon, he unhitched the two animals and got the fire going to cook beans and salt pork for supper. The men would be hungry once they got the cattle settled down and the horses hobbled.

SIXTEEN

❧

Dodge City

Three weeks later, the crew was hunkered around the fire finishing up their breakfast and drinking coffee.

"Any more bacon?"

"Naw, but there's sinkers and lick." Will had picked up the cowboy slang for biscuits and molasses.

Jake filled the crew's cups and poured himself another cup of coffee. "Dodge City's coming up in a couple days," he said, looking at each man in the crew to get their attention. "After we get loaded up, ya'll get your pay. Then ya're free to do whatever's on your mind. Just remember that Dodge City's a wild town. I recommend pullin' in your horns when ya run into some of the tough hombres here. Otherwise, ya'll end up in Boot Hill."

"If some of ya are on the dodge because of some trouble in Fort Worth, don't let anyone get ya riled." Jake looked directly at Will who quickly busied himself putting away plates and the Dutch oven from breakfast.

Will knew he needed to keep his ear to the ground to find out if anyone was on his trail. It had been almost two months now. He wasn't sure it was safe yet to head back home, although he hoped it was. There was his sour gut again. The guilt he felt about leaving Delia plagued him. He could hear her scolding him for leaving her when she was about to deliver their sixth child. At night on the trail, he tossed without sleep thinking about her. He imagined her trying to take care of the little ones and wondered if the older boys were helping. How was she managing alone without him?

Still, despite his worries, there were things he enjoyed about this life. In addition to being the dough wrangler, he had earned the respect of the cowboys by serving as the banker or by doctoring their injuries. Cooking for the men was simpler than raising hogs and chickens, but he missed Delia and her soft body spooning next to him at night. "I hope she'll forgive me" he muttered to himself.

Will was familiar with the reputation of Dodge City as a tough town where money flowed easily and men could lose it just as easily. He had already decided not to gamble. He knew he couldn't afford to lose any money. He also knew arguments were often settled with a gun. He needed to avoid any more gunfights.

It was past sunset when the cattle were all loaded into rail cars outside of town a couple of days later. The crew had been paid and had headed into town. Will was watchful as he ambled down Main Street with Jake and Tom. They were going to a saloon for whiskey to wash down the day's grime.

Jake teased him, "Anxious, Cookie? Ya keep

turning around and lookin'.'"

"He's worried that one of those gunslingers like Bat Masterson might shoot him in the back." Tom added.

"I'm just excited," Will lied. "Never been to this famous town, but I've heard plenty of stories about gunslingers like Masterson and Wyatt Earp. Wonder if we'll see em."

The center of town was lively with cowboys, gunslingers, gamblers, outlaws and railroad men bragging about their exploits on the street, moving in and out of the saloons to buy a drink, and flirting with the fancy dressed women in the dance halls. The streets were dusty trails with an occasional board sidewalk. Will could hear the honky-tonk music, men shouting across the rutted street and the occasional light-hearted laughter of a calico queen. The excitement was not reflected in the buildings, which looked crudely thrown together with rough unpainted wood. They walked past graves marked by pieces of wood stuck in the ground, some with a name scrawled on them, but many had no marker at all. A lonely ending for gunfighters buried with their boots on. Will shuddered as he thought about the risk for him. He, too, could end up in Boot Hill.

The three men strode through the swinging doors at the Long Branch Saloon. It was crowded and noisy. The air smelled of stale smoke and whiskey. From a corner of the hall, the sound of the piano floated over the voices. The other wranglers from their crew had been here a while, drinking and playing billiards at the back of the room. They shouted and cheered and booed each other as the ball dropped into a pocket. Will and his two companions elbowed their way up to the bar and ordered whiskeys.

Will hurriedly downed his first drink and ordered another before surveying the crowd. He noticed a man with a knife scar across his left cheek at the other end of the bar; he was intently watching the crew at the billiard tables. He wore a black hat pulled down to the middle of his forehead. He had a gun holstered on both hips. His bushy mustache grew down on either side of his mouth which was stretched in a tight grimace. He scowled as he looked over each man from the drive and then down at a piece of paper on the bar.

Will inched over to Jake. "Who's the tough hombre at the other end of the bar?"

"Looks like a bounty hunter. I'll go find out." Jake picked up his whiskey and approached the man who continued to look over the individual members of the crew. He hadn't appeared to have spotted Will and his two friends.

"Lookin' for someone?" Will heard Jake ask. "That's my crew you're watchin'." Jake jerked his thumb towards the billiard table. Will couldn't hear the stranger's reply.

When Jake returned, Will had moved into the shadows to be less conspicuous. He wanted to be near the back door so he could make a quick escape.

"He's looking for a gambler dressed as a hayseed." As Jake relayed his conversation, Will's heart raced. "Had a gunfight and killed some upstanding citizen in

Fort Worth. Reported to have joined a cattle drive. This tough cowboy's a bounty hunter, looking over our crew for a 'Will Martin.'"

Will glanced quickly toward the back door.

"I told him we had no Will Martin on our crew," Jake said firmly.

But as Jake reassured him, Will felt a gun barrel pressed into his ribs. "Don't move, Martin, or you're deadwood. We know you killed a man back in Fort Worth. Saw the poster. We're goin' to collect the bounty." Will recognized the two men from the crew who'd made him feel uneasy.

SEVENTEEN

Tied Up

When Will regained consciousness, he found himself tied to a chair in a dark room. He tried to move his arms but they were tied so tightly behind him that the rope cut into his wrists. His face hurt. The bandana in his mouth was knotted around his head. His jaw hurt horribly, he wondered if it was broken.

They must have knocked me pretty hard, he thought. Now what? The sour taste of panic rose in his throat. He tried to move his body, rocking back and forth until he pushed so hard he tipped himself over. As he lay there trying to determine how he was going to get himself upright, he heard movement outside the door.

The door crashed open. It was the bounty hunter from the Long Branch Saloon. With a mocking laugh, he looked down at Will. "Well, hello, Martin. Nice of your fellow wranglers to tie ya up for me." He set Will upright and took off the bandana from his mouth.

Will moved his jaw tenderly. A pain shot up to his right temple. "What are you going to do?" he muttered.

"I'm taking ya back to Fort Worth to collect the

bounty on your head for killing that sucker. But first, I'm going to get ya over to the jail for the night. I want to be sure your friends don't take care of ya first. We'll travel in the morning."

The man removed some of the ropes around Will then he handcuffed and blindfolded him. As another sharp pain shot up the side of Will's head, the bounty hunter left the room, saying, "Don't try to go anywhere. I'm just checking if the coast is clear."

Will's breath was short and shallow and his heart was pounding. How could he get out of this?

The bounty hunter returned, cut loose the ropes that tied Will to the chair and yanked him up on his feet. "Don't try any tricks, Martin. I am bigger and tougher than ya." Will felt the coldness of a gun against his ribs.

A few minutes later, he was sitting in a jail cell. He was no longer cuffed and the blindfold was removed. It was very dark and he couldn't see much but he could sense that he was in the cell alone. The stench from the unemptied slop pail was sickening. He heard voices.

"No, sir. I won't let anyone in to see 'em. No sir." Must be the jailer, Will thought.

The bounty hunter's voice was loud and firm, "I'll be back just before daybreak to get him. Got to get me another horse to put him on." He paused a moment. Then he growled, "Remember, I'll kill ya if you let anyone in and he gets away." Will heard the door slam.

Will felt hopeless. He slumped down to the floor and let his chin fall to his chest. But then he thought he heard something outside the barred window. He got up and went closer.

"Psst, Cookie. Listen, be alert when he comes back."

"We're waiting for him."

It was Jake and Tom. He took a deep breath and whispered back. "Ready. Ho."

The wait dragged into hours. He heard the jailer snoring. He watched the sky out the small window and paced back and forth. When he saw streaks of light, he knew the time was imminent. He listened for any sounds to give him clues. Voices in the distance. The neighing of a horse. Finally, footsteps and the door to the jail opened. A voice demanded, "Hey 'John Law' open up that cell. We're here to take Mr. Martin."

He let out a breath and smiled. He knew that voice. Then, voices were arguing, scuffling, a body fell. More thumps and scuffling. Another crash against the wall. Then quiet. The jangle of keys and his cell door was open. He was blindfolded, a rope dropped around him pinning his arms and led outside.

"Hurry! Get up on that horse. And hang on." He didn't recognize that voice. His horse took off following the others galloping like the devil was after them. After about an hour, they pulled up. He was ordered off the horse, the rope loosened and his blindfold removed.

Will looked around. They were in a gulley hidden from the prairie by a stand of tall grass. The sky was light. The sun was coming up over the eastern horizon. He looked at the three men staring at him with bandanas over their faces. He recognized Jake and Tom sitting on their mounts. Their eyes were crinkled at the edges. They were smiling.

But who was the third man standing next to his horse holding his bandana and curling the rope that had tied him up?

"Hello, Cookie, I'm Mort." Ah, the unknown voice he'd heard. "I'm a pal of Tom's here. He told me a friend of his needed help so I signed on. He tells me ya saved his skin a couple of times on this drive. Anyone who does that becomes a friend of mine too."

Jake spoke up now. "We needed a third man to get ya out of there who knows this territory." He handed Will a pack. "Here's some food, cooking supplies and clothes. Your pay's in the bottom. Ya'll also need these," he added, giving Will a Colt with holster and ammunition and a rifle. "Your horse's name is Stripe. He's strong and fast. One of the best from the remuda."

Tom pulled the handkerchief from his face and grinned at Will. "I think we're even now." Then he tossed a hat in Will's direction. "Shade your face. It's pretty ugly."

Will reached up to touch his jaw and winced. He attached his supplies to the saddle and put on his holster and swung up on his horse. Why had these men rescued him?

Soon, as Tom had advised, Will was heading north, keeping the cattle trail in sight. Jake, Tom and Mort had all headed off in different directions to circle back into town.

EIGHTEEN

The Kansas Prarie

Will had been riding for three days now, stopping at night and camping in protected draws or along creeks shaded by cottonwoods. He kept looking over his shoulder and swept the horizon with his eyes. The land was vast and unclaimed by homesteaders, covered in thick buffalo grass reaching as high as the underbelly of his horse.

He was grateful for the horse Jake had given him. Stripe was strong and fast. He had gotten his name because of the light stripe down the front of his face, which stood out against the rest of his medium brown coat. Will had seen Tom ride Stripe, cut out and race to the front of the herd to catch the lead steer. Now he was relying on Stripe's stamina and energy for the long days of traveling.

Will rode slumped in the saddle, pondering his situation. If it weren't for Jake and Tom, he'd be in the custody of the bounty hunter or maybe those two crooks from the trail crew. He reached up and hesitantly touched his face where they'd hit him. It was still sore and swollen, but it was healing. He shuddered as he thought about what was waiting for him in Fort Worth. He admitted to himself reluctantly that he couldn't go home to Texas now and he began to sort through the alternatives. Maybe he would go as far as Iowa. Or even back to Indiana. As he considered this, Delia's image appeared before him, pleading, "Don't go."

I'm sorry I let you down, Delia, he thought to himself. You'll have to figure out how to get by on your own. I can't help you now.

A nearby movement startled him from his reverie and he looked up to see a band of antelope bounding gracefully through the grass. As he considered bagging one, he imagined the smell of frying meat sizzling over the fire and the strong greasy flavor in his mouth. His mouth watered and he realized he was hungry. The pain in his jaw had kept him from swallowing much of the trail food that Jake had packed for him.

Before he could reach for his rifle, both he and Stripe heard the buz-z-z from a rattler laying nearby in the sun. Stripe stumbled backward into a prairie dog hole. He seemed about to fall and take Will with him, but the horse was able to right himself at the last second. Unfortunately, when he began walking ahead again, it was clear he was limping. Will dismounted and led Stripe slowly over to a small spring and stream near a stand of young trees. The water flowed over smooth pebbles that covered the bottom. The nesting birds sang as if they were welcoming them.

After Stripe had a long drink, Will examined the horse's leg. He was relieved to find that it was a minor injury and that although Stripe was limping, he could put weight on it. With some rest, it would heal. This cool glen would allow them both to heal and rest up, hopefully unseen, for a couple of days. Will hobbled his horse and climbed up a nearby rise to take a look. The prairie stretched unbroken into the distance. He was relieved to see no sign of a single human being, no buildings, no fences, only another band of antelope dancing across the horizon. He decided to try his hand at hunting.

Unfortunately, he had no success. The antelope seemed to know where he was and move just beyond his range. He was on foot so he didn't want to get too far away from his camp and his injured horse. So he turned back frustrated and empty-handed. On his return, however, he was rewarded with an abundance of wild purple plums growing on the bushes in one of the draws. Untying his bandana from around his neck, he made it into a sling and filled it with as many of the sweet plums as it would hold. They were a tasty addition to his sparse supper of beans with salt pork. Vowing to try again to bag an antelope tomorrow, he fell asleep dreaming of the smell of wild game sizzling over the fire.

The next day, he rose early, appreciating the stillness of the morning and not needing to look over his shoulder. He hiked west this time, hoping he would catch a herd at their early morning watering hole. Quietly he reached the top of a rise and carefully looked around a large boulder and over the edge. There was a small herd of about twelve or fifteen does grazing on the tender grass and drinking from the creek at the bottom of the canyon. A buck waited off to the side surveying the territory and watching for predators.

What a rack of antlers he carried! Will raised his rifle and sighted on the nearest animal, a doe. As the shot reverberated off the rocks, the herd bounded away. Will was pleased as he watched the doe fall.

He spent most of the day dressing the animal. He hung strips up to smoke near the fire, hoping to dry them out enough for jerky before he moved out. He would eat the prime cuts fresh over the next few days. For now, he could smell the mouth-watering steaks cooking over the fire. His jaw was healing. He was ready for a tasty feast. But his anticipation was spoiled when he heard a twig crack behind him. Stripe's ears perked up.

"Okay, mister. Who are you and what are you doing on my land?" An adolescent boy holding a rifle at Will emerged from behind a tree. His face was shaded by a battered straw hat, leaving visible only the set straight line of his mouth and the clenched muscles of his jaw. He wore ragged cut-off pants held up with suspenders, scuffed boots and a faded blue shirt that was several sizes too big. He was young and small. Maybe, about twelve or thirteen.

Will stuttered his reply as he instinctively raised his arms. "I.. I'm ju.. .just r… riding through. I don't mean no harm. My horse's lame… I wanted to give him time to heal up. Is this really your land?"

"Oh, so you don't think I could homestead out here by myself?" The youth's voice was filled with indignation. "Well, it's my family's land. And we don't put up with no trouble on it. I'll give you a couple of days. Then you'd better scram."

When Will noticed that the boy's hands were shaking,

he relaxed. With his final defiant message, "I don't want no trouble," the young man scrambled over some downed trees and rocks and hurried north across the prairie. Will briefly wondered where the boy lived since he hadn't seen any signs of habitation for miles. Then a worrying thought crossed his mind. What if the boy decided to tell the law about Will?

Will watched the young man recede as the sun began to drop into the grasslands. There was something a little odd about that boy. Something just didn't add up. But his hunger got the better of him and he turned to the fried venison steak and pulled it off the fire. This had to be the best steak he had ever eaten, especially with a few wild plums thrown in the pan. He gobbled it up, eating with his hands and tearing off hunks of meat like a coyote. He smacked his lips as he sopped up the grease and wipe the pan clean with the final bite of the stale biscuit he found in his trail food pack from Tom. His hunger satisfied, he stretched out next to the fire and stared up at the stars until he fell into a deep and dreamless sleep.

NINETEEN

Checking It Out

Will's curiosity and worry about his visitor were getting the better of him and the next day he decided to walk in the direction the kid had taken yesterday. After hiking for a couple of hours, he came upon a copse of trees. Hiding behind a large cottonwood tree, he looked around and noticed a rough wooden door in what looked like a mound of dirt piled against some rocks. Next to the door a bunch of prairie flowers were stuck in a jar. Nearby, stood a hay crib, a couple of milk cows in rough stalls, and a low structure that seemed to be a chicken coup without any chickens. He waited, hoping to catch a glimpse of the boy, but after waiting for a long time and seeing no sign of him or anyone else, Will turned around and hiked back to his camp.

A couple of days later, Will decided he'd ride by the homestead when he headed out. Perhaps he'd see the young man and let him know he was leaving. That night, as he stretched out by the fire, he pictured the boy holding the rifle on him. Suddenly he sat up. The young man wasn't a man; he was a young woman dressed as a boy. Now it all made sense: prairie flowers, the delicate hands shaking as she held the gun; the fine features peeking out from under the hat. But the real giveaway was how she walked. No man walked from the waist down and swung his hips side to side.

The next day, Will rode northwest, taking it slowly. In part because he wanted to protect Stripe and avoid another injury, but also because he wanted to give the young "man" a chance to see him leaving. He rode up to the trees near the homestead, boldly dismounted and let Stripe drink at the creek while he filled his canteen.

"Hi, Mister, what's your name?"

Will turned to see a little girl about four with a round impish face and large eyes the color of cinnamon. Her thin blond hair stuck out from under her frayed green sunbonnet. She wore a blue gingham dress several sizes too big that was pinned up at the waist.

"Ma said I shouldn't talk to any strange men who came by. But I don't always do what she says. Tell me your name," she demanded.

Will glanced around. Was she alone? Should he give her his real name? He knew it was common practice among cowboys to give what they called a "summer" or fictitious name.

"My name's Sam. What's yours?"

"Margaret Ann."

"That's a big name for such a little girl."

"Well, you have a little name for a big man. What's the name of your horse?"

"His name is Stripe. You know why?"

"Cause he has a stripe on his face. He has a little

name for a big horse. Are you going to stay with us?"

At that moment, a voice called, "Margaret Ann! Get back in here." Margaret Ann turned around and ran off through the trees.

As Will watched her disappear into the ground near a pile of rocks, he found himself thinking about his own two little girls. He turned away, his eyes prickling with tears as he pictured them skipping over the dirt path between the house and the barn back in Texas. He wondered how they were getting along without him.

Lost in his reverie, he didn't hear her approach. She was no more than five feet away from him when he turned around. She wore the same clothes as when he'd seen her three days earlier, but the straw hat was pushed back and her thick honey-colored hair fell to her shoulders. Now, it was obvious she was a woman, with her gently pointed nose, high cheek bones, and smooth tanned skin. Her pewter eyes were luminous and lined with long dark lashes. She assessed him with a head-to-toe once-over and then met his eyes.

"So your name's Sam. You moving out like I asked?" With her sharp tone, Will could feel his defenses rising. But her gaze drew him in and he was curious to learn more about her.

"Yes, ma'am. But before I ride off, could I get a cup of coffee?" He longed for a cup of coffee—he hadn't had one since Dodge. But he was even more interested in her. She seemed to be living alone with her daughter. He wondered how she'd got here and how she managed by herself.

She hesitated before her lips parted and a smile spread

across her face, crinkling her eyes. "I'd be happy to give you a cup of coffee," she said.

Will felt his heart speed up and his stomach flutter. "Thank you, ma'am. I'll be riding on after the coffee."

She turned and motioned him to follow her down the trail. After tying up Stripe on the fence rail, Will watched as she poured coffee into two cups from a pot sitting on the coals in the fire pit. Nearby was a bucket of water, a blackened skillet and cook pan, some plates, cups and utensils all neatly stacked on the dried buffalo grass mat. Her hands shook a little as she handed him a cup.

"We live outside most of the time," she said. "Only use the dugout at night and when it's too cold. Have a seat on that mat. Sorry, it's not fancy but maybe it's more comfortable than the hard ground."

"Thanks, ma'am. Beats the ground and maybe even my saddle." Will struggled to contain his eagerness by taking a sip of coffee. He drank the rest of the cup thoughtfully, only speaking again when he was done. "You know, we didn't start off on the right foot. Let's begin again. How'd ya do, my name is Sam. I don't believe I have the pleasure of knowing your name."

She grinned as she shook his offered hand. "Peggy. Pleased to meet you."

Will smiled. "Likewise. I've met Margaret Ann already. You've other children, a husband?"

Peggy hesitated. When she replied, her voice was barely audible. "I have two children left. Two died before my husband, Howard. Margaret Ann's older brother, Simon, is out collecting cow chips and kindling for the fire.

I'm hoping I don't lose them, too."

Will searched for the right words but all he could think of to say was, "I'm sorry."

Peggy's eyes glistened as she looked out over the swaying prairie grass. She sat motionless, holding herself tightly. Will took the last swig from his cup, stood and reluctantly offered, "I'd better mosey on so I can ride a piece today."

Peggy jumped up. "No, you don't need to leave yet. Can't you visit a bit, stay for dinner and ride out this afternoon? You're the first person that has come by here for over a year. It would be nice to have someone else to talk to for a bit." Will hesitated. He was drawn to her and she seemed lonely. But he needed to put more distance between him and Dodge City.

"Tell you what," she said. "I need some help fixing that corral for the horses. There are posts and materials near the barn. We got them on the last trip to town before Howard died. If you can do that this morning, I'll fix you a good antelope dinner at mid-day and you can ride a ways until sunset."

As the morning heated up, Will was digging post holes, regretting he had let her charm him into staying. He worried he was setting himself up for trouble again. If she hadn't beamed that smile at him, he could have said no to that antelope dinner. He could cook himself a tasty supper, after all.

He had one post hole left to dig when Margaret Ann came skipping over to the corral to announce that he should come for dinner. The sun was high in the cloudless azure sky. Will's mouth watered as the aroma wafted toward him.

Antelope steaks sizzled over the fire, burning hot from the "prairie coal," the cow chips used as fuel for cooking fires. Peggy offered him a plate with a large steak and two slices of thick bread to sop up the juice from the meat. Simon was huddled near Peggy. His hair and eyes were nut brown and he had the same long lashes as Peggy. Will sat on his haunches, cut up his meat, and swallowed his food in gulps with few words while Simon peaked at him surreptitiously and Margaret Ann sat across from him and stared.

When he was wiping up the last of the meat juice on his plate with a piece of bread, she asked, "Why do you sit like that?"

"Because this is how cowboys sit. Cowboys are heel squatters"

"You don't look like a cowboy."

"How do cowboys look?"

"Cowboys look mean and shoot people."

"That's enough, Margaret Ann," Peggy said.

Simon was still sitting quietly snuggled up next to Peggy, picking at the food on his plate. Will decided he looked to be six or seven.

Will caught him shyly peeking at him again. "How old are ya, Simon?"

He buried his face in his mother's lap. "Are you six? Seven?" Peggy said. Simon shook his head. "Then how old are you?"

He raised his head and whispered, "Eight."

Will could barely hear him and, with a wide grin, he asked, "Are you ten?"

"No," Simon offered, grinning back now. "I'm eight."

Will was surprised. Peggy explained, "Simon's small for his age. He's been sick several times. But he's learning to be strong. Aren't you?" She looked at him as if willing him to grow into a sturdy, resilient nine-year-old. Simon grinned then shyly ducked his head behind Peggy's arm.

Peggy turned back to Will. "How did you do with the post holes?"

Will noticed that her gray eyes had deep shimmering shadows. She was studying him, still on her guard. Then her mouth curled up in a smile and her face seemed to glow.

"Just one left," he said. "I'll finish it after dinner and then hit the breeze."

"Where are you headed?" Peggy asked. "And how did you happen to be out here on the Kansas prairie anyway? No one comes this way." A worried frown passed over her forehead.

"Aw, I'm exploring. Maybe headed to new territory. Not sure yet. Like I said, I'll finish the post holes now and head out."

TWENTY

❧

Staying On

*H*e didn't leave that afternoon. He finished the post holes and then decided to finish the corral. The task took several days. He worked hard and each night slept in the shed on a bed of straw, reminding himself before he fell asleep that he should move on. But Peggy needed more help reinforcing the sod shed for the animals, picking corn, digging up potatoes and corraling the cattle. He was reassured by Margaret Ann and Peggy telling him more than once that they hadn't seen another person in over a year. The isolation he found here on her homestead seemed a good exchange for the work he was doing. As more time passed, he relaxed and found himself anticipating the enjoyment of meals with Peggy and her children.

Still, he also worried about Delia and his children. Was the new baby healthy? He hoped his older children were helping Delia care for the younger ones. Guilt brought tears to his eyes when he saw how difficult it was for Peggy to take care of the homestead. How could Delia manage their small farm and be a mother to their six children? She needed him too. But he was afraid to return to Texas. If he was arrested he'd be no good to Delia or the children. It seemed far wiser to stay here.

Will remained there until fall when, one day, after little Simon laid down on the grass mat by the fire and fell asleep, Peggy couldn't get him to wake up. She asked Will to carry him into the dugout. When he picked him up, Will realized he was burning up. Will tried using his cook's knowledge of herbs and treatments to help the frail boy. He mixed up cream of tartar, ground cloves and molasses and told Peggy to give Simon a teaspoonful three times a day. But Simon went from burning hot with fever to chills that shook his fragile body. He wrapped his skinny arms tightly around Peggy's neck for warmth and comfort, and although he was bundled in blankets he turned blue. A week after he got sick, the little boy rested his head on his mother's shoulder for the last time.

Will dug through the prairie sod, preparing a grave up on the hill next to Simon's Pa and his two older brothers. Peggy retreated to the dugout.

For weeks afterward, Peggy sat on the only chair in the dugout without fire or light, silently rocking back and forth. Will remembered his own mother sitting in a rocking chair after his Pa died, silent, unaware that anything else existed. The childhood memories of his own loss and isolation filled him with grief. His loneliness seemed to expand inside his chest, threatening to suffocate him. He longed for Delia, to feel her warm body next to him and to see his children. His guilt of leaving them without support gnawed at his gut. He was ready to go home, but he told himself that he couldn't leave Margaret Ann, not with

Peggy grieving so severely. Then, as he reflected more, he admitted to himself he was also staying because he wanted to be near Peggy.

Will wanted to comfort her, but he also knew that he should maintain distance; Peggy was an independent lady and he was still a married man. To handle his emotions, he often rode out and stayed away for long days. Carefully sweeping his sight across the horizon, he searched the prairie for signs of other homesteaders or riders. One day he came upon a homestead in the distance, but he saw no evidence of people. Not wanting to encounter anyone, he galloped away.

When he returned, he'd entertain Margaret Ann with stories from the cattle drive. She was always excited to see him and he relished her enthusiastic jump into his arms upon his return. Some days he took her with him to explore, explaining to her about the seasons, the weather, pointing out plants and landmarks to mark their way back to the homestead.

One bitterly cold night a couple of months after Simon died, Will had taken some stones from the fire to the shed to provide him some warmth. He was just getting settled with his blanket roll on the pile of the buffalo grass he used as a mattress when he saw the lantern bobbing toward the shed. It was Peggy wrapped in the familiar oversized jacket which overwhelmed her small frame.

"Sam, it's too cold for you to sleep out here," she said. "You'll freeze. You can sleep in the dugout. The coals in the stove keep it warm inside."

"No, it's not right. I can't do that."

"You can sleep on the extra mat," she offered flatly. Will knew that it was her husband's mat.

That night, as he fell asleep on the mat in the dugout listening to Peggy breathe on the other mat. Remembering that Peggy had called him Sam, he realized he no longer thought of himself as Will. He was Sam Martin now; he'd left Will Martin and his life on the run behind.

TWENTY-ONE

Seasons on the Homestead

Through the bitter winter nights, Sam slept in the dugout, usually going in after Peggy and Margaret Ann were asleep and rising early to get the fire going. He was happy to be in the dugout when a terrible early spring blizzard raged for three days. The air was sharp and brittle. The wind roared, sweeping across the land under a lead gray sky. He rode out on Stripe to gather in as many of the cattle as he could find and get them into the corral. After working to get hay for them, he was chilled to the bone and his stiff fingers had no feeling. He stumbled toward the dugout but the snow was falling so thick he couldn't find his way.

"Sam, Sam, over here. Where are you?" He turned sharply to the right and floundered toward Peggy's voice. Finally, he felt the rough solidness of the door frame, her hands reaching for him. He tumbled inside.

The three of them spent three days inside, melting snow for water and keeping the dugout warm enough by feeding cow chips into the stove. By the second day, Peggy and Margaret Ann began asking him questions about his past.

"Sam, you've never told me what you were doing before... before you stopped off here?"

He grinned. "I was riding across the Kansas prairie. My horse was lame after he stepped in a prairie dog hole. Then this young kid ordered me off 'his' land."

She laughed. "No, seriously, what were you doing before you were riding across the prairie?"

"I worked a cattle drive as the cook."

"Why did you leave?" Margaret Ann wanted to know.

"Oh, I wanted to try something new, explore new territory."

"Where do you want to go?" asked Margaret Ann. "Where is a territory?"

"Territory is where there aren't any people. I want to explore just like you and I did before the cold and snow came when I took you out on Stripe."

"But, why can't you stay here and explore? There aren't any other people here. I want you to stay here."

Anxious to change the subject, Sam said, "I haven't heard the story about how you came to be living by yourself on this homestead."

Sadness crossed Peggy's face. "I guess I can talk about it now. Howard and I were married in Iowa, near Monrovia. We both grew up there. We farmed some land his father owned. The boys were all born in Iowa. We scrimped and saved so we could get our own place. We came out here with all our things in one wagon pulled by two oxen. We took turns riding the two horses and walking. Even Simon. We didn't have much but the wagon was so full there wasn't room to ride. We eventually traded the oxen for milk cows.

Howard wanted land near a spring. He and another fellow, Burt, who joined us on the trail, found this land. We filed our claims. But Burt wanted to go further west. He headed out a few months later."

"How long have ya been here?" Sam wanted Peggy to keep talking. He liked listening to her smooth voice.

Peggy looked at Margaret Ann. "She was born right after Howard finished the dugout... so just four years."

"How long have you been alone?" There was a long silence. Margaret Ann snuggled up next to her mother. Sam worried that he had over-stepped. Peggy stared at a spot on the wall, the dim light of a candle casting deep shadows on her face. Finally, in a hollow voice, her lips barely moving, she said, "The older boys got sick from the fever the first year we were here. Howard died in the winter last year. He had gone out to get the cattle just as a blizzard like this one was moving in. I went out to find him when the snow let up. He must have fallen and hit his head. He froze to death."

Peggy was quiet and looked so vulnerable. Sam put an arm around Peggy's shoulders. "What a hard blow for ya." She looked at him as a weak smile crossed her face. He wanted to wrap both of his arms around her to comfort her but she leaned away from him. He realized more contact at this time was not welcome.

As the days began to warm, the snow was melting and spring seemed near. Sam knew it was time to pull up stakes. Yet, he wanted to stay.

Peggy seemed more relaxed and not as distant since their exchange during the blizzard. She occasionally reached out and touched his arm. The previous week, she had laughingly offered, "If you stay, work the cattle and help with planting the garden this spring, I'll make you a part owner."

He felt her sitting next to him at the fire in the evening. He was tempted to move closer, reach out and touch her, kiss her and take her in his arms. He longed to feel her body next to his, to find the physical comfort and acceptance he yearned for. His desire clouded his reason. Yet, he knew it wasn't right. And her offer of part ownership was, after all, just a business proposition.

As the days warmed he sat alone one morning by the fire drinking his first cup of coffee at the edge of dawn, his favorite time of day. Here on the prairie with the wind unusually still, he could see what seemed like the edges of the earth as he looked around in all directions. The rock behind the trees at the fresh water spring was dark, outlined with the light behind it. He could see it clearly through their bare branches. Looking in the other direction, he could see the prairie was splashed with patches of snow amidst the dried brown buffalo grass. Looking up, he saw a sliver of moon as the sky turned from gray to lavender. Then, the sun emerged like a huge glowing fireball, flooding the sky with orange light. The meadowlarks began their serenade and the deer stepped up to the spring for their morning drink. Nature seemed to be reassuring him that his secret was safe here.

He took another gulp of coffee and shook his head to clear his thoughts.

He needed to hit the trail. But in which direction?

Back to Texas and Delia? Would she even take him back almost a year after he'd left? Maybe better to strike out on his own to Wyoming or north to Montana where no one knew him.

He was on the verge of finalizing his decision when Peggy asked, "Would you stay a little longer to help bring the cattle in and expand the vegetable garden? Then you can leave."

Sam couldn't say no. So, he stayed on to help collect the cattle that they had let roam over the prairie during the harsh winter. He began to dig up sod to enlarge the vegetable garden near the natural spring. But he struggled to hold his feelings back. He was still a wanted man and he was married to Delia. He couldn't bear to do anything that would hurt Peggy or Margaret Ann. As it warmed up, he moved back to the shed to sleep.

"Why are you moving out?" Peggy asked. "You can stay in the dugout. It's fine with me. You've been a gentleman." She seemed oblivious to his attraction to her.

"It's just not right," he responded as he turned and carried his mattress to the shed. If he stayed he didn't think he could continue to be the gentleman that Peggy thought he was.

On clear nights, he lay outside to watch the pale sky, washed out by the sun, turn to a rich dark blue canopy. He counted the stars as they began to glitter until there were just too many to count. The crickets raised their voices in loud crescendo and the frogs up at the spring called for their mates. With nature's music in the background, he reviewed his options, again.

He would like to stay in this out-of-the-way place where he could hide from the law. He would like to stay indefinitely with Peggy, be a father to Margaret Ann, who had captured his heart. Peggy was easy to be around; they had fun together and laughed a lot. She appreciated whatever he did around here. Peggy wasn't clingy or demanding. She knew how to accept life and move on. In fact, sometimes she was too self-reliant.

But there was a catch if he stayed here. Could he be with her and not be honest about his life? Several times already, he had come close to telling her. For sure, she wouldn't want him if she knew he was still married to another woman, let alone on the dodge from the law.

He should just head back to Texas with the hope that Delia would take him back. His guilt about abandoning his children left a sour taste whenever he thought about them.

Finally, he made his decision. Now he just needed to find the right time to talk with Peggy.

TWENTY-TWO

Caught Off Guard

The next morning, Peggy and Margaret Ann climbed out of the dugout earlier than usual. Sam was still starting the fire and putting on the coffee. This was his chance to tell her.

"Hey, Sam are you burning that coffee again?" She laughed, turning on her biggest smile and touching him on the arm. "You've been so generous and helpful. Margaret Ann and I like having you around. And, I have another favor. I just know you'll do it for us." She blinked her long lashes at him.

"Uh, oh." He took a step back in mock resistance, laughing, as he thought how easily she pulled him in.

"We want a house. We're tired of living in the ground. That last downpour did it with the mud falling in on us! We can't build it by ourselves. I know you're the right person to help us. Now, you can't say 'no' to both of us, can you?

"I can sell some cattle so we can buy the supplies we need. It doesn't have to be big, just two or three rooms for now. We'll help, but we can't do it alone. I'll even pay you or give you some cattle. Just tell me what it will take." She paused to catch her breath, looking at him with her luminous gray eyes. "So you'll help us, right?"

"Whoa! You need to take a breath," Sam said. "What made you decide this right now?"

It seemed such a strange coincidence that Peggy should ask for this favor just when he had finally decided to move on.

"We didn't decide just now." She turned to look and smile at Margaret Ann. "We've been talking about it every time the rain leaks into the dugout or when we were shut up in that dark hole with the blizzard howling above us. We need a house with some windows and a strong roof. I know you can do this for us. You can't leave just yet. Wherever you're going can wait a little longer, can't it?"

"Besides, I want you to stay," Margaret Ann chimed in.

Sam smiled at Margaret Ann and then at Peggy, amused at her rehearsed plea and wondering what it was she really wanted from him. But he couldn't say no, she was right about that.

"Sure, let's talk after breakfast about which cattle to take into town to be sold. Then we can make plans for this house you're dreaming about."

She jumped up, threw her arms around his neck and kissed him right on the mouth. "Thank you! You've made us both happy." Before he could recover from the sparks that went off inside, Margaret Ann jumped into his arms to give him her own hug with a kiss on his cheek, knocking his hat to the ground. "Thanks, Mr. Sam. I knew you'd do it!"

TWENTY-THREE

Going Into Town

Sam wiped his brow again. Was it the sun heating up the prairie or was the sweat from his worry about who he would meet in Dodge City? He hoped that the bounty hunters would be looking for the latest wanted outlaw instead of him.

He had tried to talk Peggy into staying home with Margaret Ann, telling her that Dodge City is no place for women and children. But she would have none of it.

"Don't talk down to me, Sam. If I'm going to make it out here, I need to know how to deal with those cowboys in town! After you leave, I'm the one who has to live with the results of this trip, not you."

"You're right," he said. "I won't be around much longer. You're gonna have to take care of yourself."

They had been on the ride south to Dodge City for two days now. Will was riding next to the lead steer to keep him going in the right direction. Peggy and Margaret Ann rode beside the last of the five cows they planned to sell. Fortunately, these cattle weren't as touchy as the Texas longhorns. If they kept the steer moving, the cows would follow.

Margaret Ann was a good little rider. She kept up a constant chatter, talking to each cow. "Hey Sally, move along. Bossy, you can't stop now. Roberta, you're a pretty girl." For her, this was a great adventure–finding a place to camp each night, building a fire to cook their evening meal and then rolling out their bed rolls to sleep next to the fire. Peggy talked with the cows, too. She believed that familiar voices would reassure them if something unusual occurred, like a sudden thunderstorm.

During the first two days they had seen no other riders. Each night, Sam relaxed a little more as he stretched out next to the fire. But soon, he knew they would see the homestead near Pawnee Creek that he'd sighted on one of his rides exploring the prairie. Inevitably, Peggy would want to ride in to say hello. For her sake, she should get acquainted with her neighbors but it might be better if he stayed in the barn with the cattle. Or perhaps his anxiety was twisting his common sense. After all, they were miles from where anyone would know him.

As they approached Pawnee Creek, a horse and rider came toward them. He was a slight young man, with a gray hat pulled down to shade his eyes. He rode easily and as he got closer he smiled and waved. His blue eyes were friendly as he called out, "Welcome to the Lazy L ranch! Where you headed?"

"Heading into Dodge City to sell these cattle," said Sam. "Mind if we set up camp here tonight?"

"Aw, come on in and join us for supper. Name's Joe"

They rode into the ranch, drove the cattle into the

corral and fed their horses. With the talk around the table, Sam discovered he had worried needlessly. Joe had come with his wife Amanda and his younger brother, Frank, from Ohio to help their uncle. The uncle "could talk the hide off a cow" as the wranglers would say. Sam didn't need to worry about any prying questions. Amanda, newly pregnant with their first child, asked Peggy if she would come back in the spring to help when it was close to her delivery date. Peggy readily agreed after getting assurance she could bring Margaret Ann.

After a generous meal, everyone gathered around an old piano and joined in singing and storytelling. Sam allowed the music to pour over him, forgetting his anxiety. Peggy's soaring soprano voice harmonized with the melody sung by the others. With urging from Peggy, he finally joined in the last song, adding his tenor voice to the harmony of "Let Me Call You Sweetheart." He avoided looking at Peggy, worried that he couldn't hide the feelings welling up in him if he did.

Listening to the singing and conversation, Sam sprawled out on the floor, as relaxed and easy as soft butter. The tension he had held in his muscles gradually eased. He let out a loud guffaw after one of the stories. He sat up when it was his turn, eager to tell his own story.

TWENTY-FOUR

Dodge City, A Second Time

A week later, in Dodge City, Sam helped Peggy negotiate a good price for her cattle, then settled her and Margaret Ann in a nice boarding house in the gun-free residential section, and headed to Front Street. He studied the wanted posters on the wall outside the Long Branch. After noticing a poster announcing that Billy the Kid had been shot in New Mexico, he saw what he'd been dreading "Wanted, William Martin" the poster said, with a reasonable picture of him, looking younger, with short hair and clean shaven. His heart raced.

As he strode away, he caught a glimpse of his image in the window... bushy black beard, his dark hair longer than in the poster, curling out from under his hat. His face was weathered and he looked much older. He was Sam Martin now.

TWENTY-FIVE

Missing in Weatherford?

They had been driving the team of horses for two long days, heading home with the lumber, nails, food and supplies on the wagon. Each night after Margaret Ann was asleep, Sam and Peggy watched the evening sky darken and the stars begin to twinkle as the campfire died down. Almost wordlessly they set out their bedrolls. One especially cool night, Peggy moved up next to his back for warmth. He kept his back to her and feigned an exhausted sleep.

The owner of the boarding house in Dodge City where Peggy and Margaret Ann had stayed raised chickens. Peggy not only bought some of the eggs for their journey but also bought a rooster and six layer hens to start a brood to replace those that had been lost during the winter when Howard had died. After cooking the last of the eggs on their way home, Sam started to throw the newspaper that had cushioned the eggs into the fire. But he paused as he studied the headlines. One said, "Low Growth in Fort Worth," and seemed to indicate that the city wasn't doing nearly as well as Dallas. The second headline he noticed was far more interesting; it said, "Tornado Levels

Weatherford,"—Weatherford being the town where he'd left Delia alone on the farm. Afraid Peggy might notice his interest, he folded it up and stuck it in his pocket to read in a private moment. It would take him some time. Though he'd gone as far as the eighth grade, it had been years since he read much.

Later, when he spread out the torn page, he was shocked to discover that the tornado had destroyed farm houses and part of the town of Weatherford. The paper had been torn through the story which referenced the farms that were damaged and people who were killed or injured. The description that remained seemed to correspond to the location near his old farm, but he wasn't sure. He read on. Several of the names listed as dead bore the same first names or initials of his wife and children, but they were incomplete and he was left not knowing if his family was hurt. He quickly stuffed it back in his pocket when Peggy approached.

That day as he rode, his thoughts were jumbled. He should have been there and now maybe it was too late. When he thought that he might never see his children again, the sadness overwhelmed him. He tried to put them out of his mind by thinking about the house Peggy wanted to build.

When he looked at the newspaper again, he discovered that on the back there was a list of the "missing and presumed dead." And there, half way down was "Delia Martin and six children." His throat closed and tears welled up in his eyes. He felt tightness and pain around his heart. His first thought was to go back to Texas. But Texas without his wife and children felt empty. And what would be the point? He might be recognized and be strung up at the end of a rope.

As they rode back toward the homestead, he was quiet. Staying with Peggy and Margaret Ann was appealing. He had strong feelings for both of them. But when he considered not having the responsibility of a wife and children, he found himself feeling light. He was drawn to being on his own and riding north or west or even back to Indiana. He would make plans to leave as soon as the house was built.

When they arrived back at the homestead late that afternoon, Sam busied himself feeding the livestock and brushing the horses. He was conscious of Peggy and Margaret Ann unloading the food supplies, arranging the cooking pots and dishes they had purchased. Soon Margaret Ann came to get him for supper. The stars came out and Margaret Ann named the constellations before she fell asleep on Peggy's lap. Sam carried her down into the dugout to her mat. Peggy followed him, put her arms around him and with a big kiss said, "I want to thank you for everything." Sam's knees went weak. He was immediately aroused. He turned to embrace her fully. As she lifted her mouth up to his, he kissed her passionately and she returned the urgency, shaking off her jacket and then clinging to him. Sam gasped for breath, engulfed by lust. He pulled her hungrily down on the mat as he surrendered, at last, to his desire.

TWENTY-SIX

Building the House

Sam woke early the next morning, rolled over and was about to gather Peggy into his arms again when he noticed Margaret Ann staring at him. Putting his finger to his lips to motion her to be quiet, he pulled on his pants and lifted Margaret Ann outside. He twirled her around as he danced next to the barely warm coals of last night's campfire. She gathered up some cow chips as he blew on the coals. As the coals turned from ashen gray to glowing red, the heat of the fire reminded him of the heat of his desire for Peggy.

He hummed, "She'll be coming 'round the mountain…" He started a pot of coffee and mixed up some sourdough biscuits.

"You're different this morning," Margaret Ann said after observing him quietly. "Why?"

"What do you mean that I'm different?"

"You're acting silly and humming. You're happy and nice. Before you were sad and kind of mean."

Sam set down his cup of coffee and lifted Margaret Ann onto his lap. "Was I mean to you?"

"No, but you made Mommy cry sometimes. So

you were mean."

"I promise. I won't be mean to your Mommy again." And he gave her a squeeze before checking on the biscuits baking in the Dutch oven.

"Is that a promise?"

Sam whirled around and grinned as he saw Peggy emerge from the dugout. She was smiling and Sam stepped toward her to wrap his arms around her.

"Good morning. Would you like some coffee?" he asked.

After a breakfast filled with giggles, stolen glances and hidden meanings, Sam and Peggy began discussing the plans for the new house. "Will you be satisfied with three rooms?"

"Yes, especially if we have a front porch where we can sit out in nice weather and watch the sun set. Let's put the window facing west and the stove at the opposite side."

"I suggest that we also make the cut outs for windows in the cooking area and in the sleeping rooms so they will be ready when ya can afford to buy glass."

"But how will we cover them?"

"I can make shutters. When it's nice ya can open them and keep them closed in cold weather."

"Where do we put the fireplace? On the side wall?"

"Yeah, I think we can make the room big enough to sit by the fire and still have a table to sit around and eat."

"That is great! I'm excited. I want a table big enough for six or eight people."

"You're going to need to get some more chairs," Sam said.

"Yes, that will come. But for now, can you make a couple of benches?"

"Sure. That's easy. Given where the fireplace will go, the doors to the two sleeping rooms will be off the opposite wall. The one for Margaret Ann will be smaller and then one for you."

"And you too, Sam." Peggy added quickly. She smiled at him. "I hope you will stay and enjoy the house when we've finished it." She leaned over and kissed him. He shuddered, ready to use that bedroom right then.

Over the next few weeks, Sam and Peggy fell into a routine of rising with the sun to work a few hours on constructing the house. During late morning and afternoon, they tended other chores, feeding the horses, checking on the cattle and weeding the garden. Margaret Ann was given the responsibility of gathering the eggs. As the day cooled off, they were back out pounding and sawing to get the walls finished. At night, they both fell onto the mats in the dugout, snuggled with happy exhaustion in each other's arms.

In a few weeks, the walls were up and they had collected brush, grass and sod to bundle with the cedar poles to cover the roof. Hurriedly, they put the roof in place, hoping to finish before a major storm moved in. Then they hung muslin sheets from the ceiling to keep the dirt and the rodents from falling into the house. Although there were many finishing touches needed inside, Peggy excitedly carried in her new chairs and stored supplies on the shelves. All three of them slept under the roof in their new sleeping rooms.

TWENTY-SEVEN

Another Winter

Since the last winter had been bitter cold, Sam predicted the coming one would be mild, not so cold or so early. "We have plenty of time before winter sets in," he assured Peggy in mid-November.

But he was wrong. The morning after that conversation, Sam was awakened early by the sound of the wind whistling around the door. The storm was a "norther," with a bitterly cold wind that almost blew him over when he stepped outside.

After breakfast, Sam peered outside again. Everything was swirling white with almost three inches of snow already on the ground. "I need to feed the horses."

"Use that rope and tie it to the post so you can find your way back. I don't want you getting lost in this white out." Peggy frowned, looking at Sam with anxiety and concern in her eyes.

"I don't need it." But outside, he couldn't see more than six inches from his face. So he grabbed the rope and tied it to the post in front of the house. He was attacked by stinging shards of ice and a hostile north wind. By the time he finished tying the rope, his fingers were stiff.

He crawled on the ground, letting the wind hurl the snow above him, inching his way toward the dark shadows that he assumed were the corral. When he got there, the horses were huddled together against the boulders that formed a protective wall. He tied the rope to the corral post.

As he stood between them patting them and murmuring reassurance, he could feel their body warmth. Their steaming breath rose and disappeared in the churning whiteness. They jostled anxiously to feed as he dumped out some precious grain for them. Then he broke the ice in the water trough with a pitchfork.

By the time he grabbed the rope to guide him back to the house, it was sheathed in ice. He could see nothing that looked familiar, only whiteness covering the ground, whirling in the air and filling the sky. He realized that without the rope he would have been lost.

When a gust of wind knocked him over, he crawled on his hands and knees, clinging to the icy rope. His clothes were stiff and frozen, his beard and mustache caked with snow and ice, and the cold bore into his bones. He could see nothing. His muscles ached. His knees were bloodied and bruised. His fingers and hands were stiff. He was exhausted and collapsed to the ground to rest, convinced he could go no further. But then he pictured Peggy and Margaret Ann waiting for him in front of the fire. Got to keep going, he thought.

He tried to get up onto his knees to crawl but his legs were so stiff they wouldn't bend. He sank to the ground again. The wind whirled around him and he tried to shield his face with his arm from the shards of ice that bombarded his head. But the arm was numb. He decided to rest just a little and try again.

He must have blanked out. Then he heard something, a woman's voice. "Sam."

I can't make it, he thought as he closed his eyes again. Then, a tug on his left arm. A second hard jerk reached past his muddled confusion. He remembered the rope he was holding.

"Sam." Peggy was calling him. He inched toward her voice, but collapsed again. Then he felt himself dragged across the frozen ground, scraping his knees and his chin.

Once she'd got him inside, Peggy pried his hand from the rope, slammed the door and closed out the wind. Much of the warmth had escaped and Sam realized she was shivering as she dragged him over to the fire to thaw out, taking care not to put him too close to the heat to prevent chilblains.

"I hope your fingers and toes aren't frostbitten," she said as she carefully removed his gloves and boots. "Margaret Ann, come over here and hold Sam's hands in yours to warm them."

Sam was touched as he watched Margaret Ann wrap her small hands around his as far as they would go. At first, he couldn't feel her hands touching his. He began to feel his face.

"Why doesn't your little finger straighten out, Sam?" Margaret Ann asked.

"Oh, it was injured when I was in the army. But I

don't miss it much now."

Soon he was drinking a hot cup of coffee. His feet tingled but he finally felt warm. He breathed a sigh of relief and returned Peggy's happy smile. Then he teased Margaret Ann that it was her turn next to go out and feed the horses.

TWENTY-EIGHT

The Winds of Spring

Spring on the prairie came overnight, it seemed. One afternoon there were patches of melting ice and snow and the next, the ground seemed almost carpeted with spring flowers. During an early spell of warm days, Sam and Peggy finished the roof on the house. Peggy began to make curtains and decorate.

"Hey, you could host President Hayes here, it looks so nice," Sam observed.

The plain wooden table he had built was decked with a nice cloth that matched the curtains at the window. In the center was the jar of spring flowers Margaret Ann had collected.

"I'm headed out to find those 'dogies' out there in the hills. Be back in a day or two dependin' on how long it takes to find 'em." Sam hugged and kissed them both good-bye then rode out to find the new calves and the cattle they had wintered in the hills. As he rode, he felt the warmth of the spring sun, smelled the fresh air gently blowing in his face, and saw the pale green emerge across the prairie almost before his eyes. He felt joy riding over the prairie with wildflowers nodding in the wind and relished the sense of contentment he felt with Peggy and Margaret Ann.

Yet, there was a snag. It was too comfortable. Something wasn't quite right. There was something else he wanted. What was it? He still felt guilty leaving Delia and the children. Less often, he thought about his mother in Indiana and wondered if she was still alive.

Did he want to get hitched again? He wasn't sure. He liked being with Peggy and enjoyed helping with the ranch, but he didn't feel responsible for its success. He could ride off anytime without obligation to Peggy and Margaret Ann.

"I won't push you," Peggy had said a few weeks earlier as they sat in front of the fireplace. "But, it would be wonderful to make us legal and give Margaret Ann a daddy."

Sam still had the itch to explore, to be able to ride off in any direction with the excitement of the unknown. That itch was gnawing at his contentment.

He enjoyed the light-hearted playfulness in his relationship with Peggy. Unlike Delia, she didn't nag or have expectations. But what if she got pregnant? His shoulders sagged. The weight of responsibility was just too heavy.

It hit him like a kick in the stomach. He needed to leave.

He rode over the next rise and discovered the cattle huddled in the draw near a stream, grazing on the new spring grass. He prompted the herd to begin plodding back to the homestead. The new unbranded calves bawled, worried they would lose their next meal, and ran skittishly to catch up with their mamas. He rode next to the lead bull to keep him moving toward home. This was an easy task.

Finding a way for him to leave the homestead required more planning.

The next evening, he was pensive. Peggy seemed concerned, breaking into his thoughts and asking, "Is somethin' wrong, Sam?"

"Huh? What? No nothin's wrong. Just tired. I'm going to go feed the horses and then go to bed."

Sam went out again the next day to collect another group of cattle with their new calves. As he herded them toward the homestead, the sun disappeared behind some steel-gray clouds. The wind whipped leaves, grass and small tree branches. He drove the cattle hurriedly into the corral. Looking up, he saw a funnel twisting in the western sky. It was a dagger descending fast.

"Peggy! Margaret Ann! A tornado! Get into the dugout!" he yelled.

Peggy was running from the garden, terror etched on her face. "Margaret Ann!" she screamed.

"Where is she?"

Peggy started for the house. "Margaret Ann!"

Sam ran after her and caught her arm. "Go to the dugout. I'll get Margaret Ann."

The sky was dark gray, almost green and the wind howled. Branches, a bucket, and poles from the corral blew past his head. He struggled to open the door. When it finally opened, the door slammed wide open against the house. The next moment, the wind pulled it off the hinges and it sailed away as if it was as light as a piece of paper. Sam clung to the door frame screaming, "Margaret Ann!" He looked around frantically. Suddenly, he was sucked into the room. He heard glass breaking and instinctively raised his arm for protection. Terrified she was hurt or blown away, he rushed to the small bedroom. "Margaret Ann!" She was crouched in the corner of the room bawling. Sam scooped her up in his arms. She buried her face in his shoulder sobbing. Flooded with relief, Sam held her close. The wind seemed to be quieting down but it was still fierce. He ran for the protection of the dugout with Margaret Ann clinging to his neck.

When it was eerily quiet and the rain had let up, Sam and Peggy went out to survey the damage. The corral and hay crib were gone and many of the cattle had taken off. The house was still standing but the door was gone, part of the roof was missing and the glass window was broken. If he was going to repair the damage, Sam realized he couldn't leave anytime soon.

But the repair, rebuilding and rounding up the cattle didn't take as long as he had feared. Joe, from the Lazy L Ranch, who was originally coming to help brand the new calves, arrived with extra poles for the corral. Although his ranch had not been touched by the tornado, he'd seen the twister in the Western sky. He had anticipated Peggy and Sam might have some damage. He offered the poles and pitched in to rebuild the corral and the hay shed and repair the damage to the house. After that, he and Sam branded the new calves.

At dinner one night, after they had started the branding, Joe asked Peggy about coming over to help Amanda who would be delivering soon. "Why don't you and Margaret Ann come back with me now? It might be a couple of weeks, but she's having a hard time and we'd really appreciate your help now."

Peggy looked surprised. "Is it time already?" But, she readily agreed. "I could be ready to leave by the day after tomorrow.?" She looked at Sam, but he avoided her gaze, instead getting up and going outside.

"Come look at the sunset!" he called. "Must be all the dust in the air."

As they all crowded around, Joe said, "It's like one of them paintings they have in the state house."

The next day, Peggy bustled around to get things ready for her departure. By the time she fell exhausted into bed, Sam was already sound asleep.

The next morning over breakfast, Margaret Ann chattered away. "I get to help with the new baby. I hope it's a girl so we can play together."

Sam went out to saddle up the horses. "Goodbye, I'll miss you both," he said as he hugged Margaret Ann and then lifted her up on her horse. He kissed Peggy, holding her longer than usual before she swung up on her horse. He stared at her back for several minutes as she rode over the rise.

TWENTY-NINE
❧

Heading North

Sam left shortly after Peggy and Margaret Ann. The first day out he headed northeast to find the old Western Cattle Trail to Ogallala. Then he headed almost due north but stayed away from the trail. Even though he'd heard in Dodge City that they weren't driving many cattle north anymore, he didn't want to risk running into anyone.

It was spring. The air was sweet. The flowers on the prairie were blooming, and the birds cheerfully sang their enjoyment of the sunshine. Sam recognized the wild columbine and the buttercups but he couldn't remember the purple flowers. Wildflowers reminded him of Peggy. He stopped to watch a hawk soaring on an updraft and then dive to the ground to catch a prairie dog for its next meal. In another day he would be out of the food he'd brought from the homestead. Better watch for some wild game. He listened to the familiar meadowlark echo across the emptiness.

Mostly he thought about Peggy. He could hear her laugh on the wind, see her infectious smile when he closed his eyes, watch her drink coffee across the campfire from him, and feel her body as he held her before she climbed on her horse. He smiled as he recalled his first encounter with the "young man" who ordered him off "his" property. He felt his blood rush when he pictured her lying next to him. He remembered her independence and persistence, qualities that evoked his admiration as well as his annoyance. He also thought repeatedly about how she would react when she returned from caring for Joe's wife and new baby and found him gone.

At first, she'll assume that I'm out rounding up cattle, he thought. He pictured her annoyance that he hadn't left a note. After a couple of days, he knew that she'd begin to worry and perhaps go out and look for him. Margaret Ann would ask where he was. Peggy might notice that he took a lot of the meat they'd dried last fall and other food from the pantry. He pictured her vacillating between hoping he would return and being so angry with him that she wouldn't want him back.

In the late afternoon, the sky turned dark, thunder rolled and lightening flashed. He took shelter in an abandoned dugout while he waited out the storm. The storm reminded him of the tornado and how frightened Margaret Ann had been. His memories of Peggy's dugout washed over him. He wanted her desperately.

He decided when the storm let up, he would turn around and ride back to the homestead. He'd let his fear of responsibility get the better of him. He shouldn't let Peggy and Margaret Ann down like this.

While he waited, it began to rain even harder. Part of the roof of the dugout gave way and dumped mud, stones and a rush of water on his head. He patched the hole using some mud and dried prairie grass that was originally there to cushion a sleeping mat. After his repair work, he reflected again on his decision to leave Peggy and Margaret Ann. He remembered that he had felt his independence being snuffed out. It was a feeling he detested. It reminded him of the forced marriage that resulted in responsibility for five children and Delia.

He shook his head to empty it of memories. He decided to focus on the future.

THIRTY

The Stranger

T he terrain had begun to change. There were more chalky outcroppings. The land was dry, almost sandy. Nothing would grow there. He remembered hearing the wranglers talking about Castle Rock, a landmark that could be seen from the Western Trail. He must be getting close. The ground here seemed to match their description.

"We need to find water, Stripe," he said. He had left a river this morning. There must be some water around Castle Rock. The drovers would have needed water for the cattle they drove north to Ogallala. He paused at an overlook and breathed a sigh of relief as he saw a river winding across the prairie in the distance. Then he saw the gleaming towers of white chalk bursting out of the flat prairie and reaching up to the sky. "Wow, what a sight!" he exclaimed. He looked around, hoping for some shade to get out of the heat. But, there was only bare land and not even enough grass to winter a prairie dog. While he let Stripe wander awhile to look for grass, he found a piece of ground without any thistles, stretched out, and shaded his eyes with his hat.

In the shimmering stillness with the mid-day sun beating down, he dozed until he felt a vibration in the ground. He scrambled up just as he caught sight of a man coming toward him. The lone rider rode a gelding and led a pack horse carrying bedrolls, saddlebags bursting with supplies, and a couple of rifles. When the rider caught sight of Sam he waved. "Hello there." His greeting echoed before it was carried off by the wind. Sam felt for his gun.

"Howdy."

"Where ya headed?" the stranger asked in a friendly tone.

"Ogallala," Sam replied as he swung up onto Stripe, trying to look casual.

"Me, too. Name's John." The stranger stuck out his hand.

Sam paused, watching the man's dark eyes inspect him from under the brim of a worn brown hat. The man's craggy face had wrinkles as deep as the Rio Grande, but his eyes twinkled and a smile played around his mouth.

"Sam. How ya' doin'?" He stuck out his hand only to find his fingers crushed by John's massive hand. Sam winced.

"Oops, sorry," John said. "I forget about my hands. By the way, I'm hoping to get to that river down there for the night. Want to join me? I'd welcome the company."

"Sure. Let's go."

They rode in silence down the narrow path. As they passed the Castle Rock, Sam commented, "That sure is some landmark. Have ya seen it before?"

"Yeah, I consider it a beacon out here in this empty

prairie. Tells me where I am and where I'm headin'." They rode in silence again until John pointed toward some trees near the river.

"Let's head over to those big cottonwoods. We can make camp there."

The shimmering leaves offered inviting shade. The trees were beginning to sprout the characteristic cottony seedpods that helped them survive the dry, hostile prairie. Between the trees, a blackened ring of rocks signaled that others had built a fire and camped under the protection of these branches.

Sam left Stripe free to graze, grabbed his rifle and hollered over his shoulder. "I'll look for some kindlin' and hope to bag somethin' for supper."

He returned later with a bunch of twigs and branches for the smoldering fire that John had already started, as well as a rabbit to roast for dinner. Later, after licking his fingers and the rabbit bones, Sam leaned back. He wanted to learn more about this stranger, to find out if he could trust him or if he had a leaky mouth.

"What's your business in Ogallala?" Sam began.

They talked well into the night, John regaling Sam with tales of his life as an itinerant preacher. Sam had taken a liking to him, enjoying his self-deprecating humor and his big barrel laugh. Still, he limited his own stories to his childhood adventures, including running away from his uncle's farm in Indiana after he was punished. As the evening wore on, he took a risk, observing John carefully as he spoke.

"A few days ago," he said, "I rode off leaving a woman,

Peggy and her daughter Margaret Ann. I stayed with them over a year. Feeling a little blue right now,"

"Your wife?"

"No. She was a widow. I've been living with them and doing chores, building a house, taking care of cattle."

"Did ya tell her you was leaving? Or did ya just ride off?"

"Oh, couldn't bear to tell her. Left on my horse while she and Margaret Ann were away helping the neighbors." Sam saw no judgment on John's expression.

"Did ya get close? Must've been hard to leave," John responded with no hint of criticism.

Sam took a deep breath. "Yeah, I miss 'em. Almost went back after a few days. Thought I must be crazy to leave a woman that wanted me, but I didn't want to get tied down. I decided to keep ridin'."

"Seems like ya prefer your freedom over the lovin,'" John said.

The sky was turning pink as the sun rose on the eastern horizon the next morning. Sam rose quietly and made his way down to the river to wash up. He left his vest, his hat and his gun belt on the bank of the river and waded in. At first, he was only going to splash water on his face and head, but the water was so refreshing and so he stripped off his clothes and lowered his whole body into the invigorating cool water. He relaxed and let the flowing water take the grime and dust accumulated since he left the "stead". As he did so, he recalled the previous night's conversation and decided he would ride along with John for the company.

THIRTY-ONE

❧

Knocked Out

Sam opened his eyes to see concern in the dark eyes staring at him. What was the smell? Reminded him of his mother.

"It's the camphor." John offered and then sat back. "Thank the Lord! Ya've come around. I was worried I was gunna to have to bury ya."

Sam tried to sit up but the trees and the ground swirled around. "Uhhh, my head," he moaned. "What happened?"

"Ya must've slipped getting out of the river and hit your head good. After I started the fire, I was wonderin' where ya were so I went a lookin'. Found ya stark naked layin' in the water at the edge of the river bank. Ya' was so still, I thought you was dead. Wrapped ya in a blanket and brought ya back to the fire. Ya started twitchin' and shakin' so I knew ya wasn't dead. I sent up a prayer of thanks."

Sam pulled up the blanket and closed his eyes. He was shivering so hard his teeth rattled. And his head felt like he had collided with a large boulder. Later, when he opened his eyes again he saw a man perched on a nearby log reading a tattered book that looked like the Bible he'd seen his mother read. The light was fading into the gray and lavender haze of evening.

Sam gingerly began to raise himself on his elbow, but pain coursed through his whole body. The man jumped up, ran over, and held him down.

"Lay still," he ordered.

Sam attempted to struggle out of the man's hold but he had no strength and fell back, breathing hard, waiting for his head to stop spinning. "Who are ya?" he demanded. "And where am I?"

John told Sam his name and explained what happened. "We met up there on the overlook and agreed to camp together here a couple of days ago. We're on the Sandy River near Castle Rock. Ya fell at the river and hit yer head pretty hard. Got pretty cold in the water laying there naked as a new born babe. Ya've been warmin' up and gettin' your strength back. I've been watchin' over ya since I carried ya up from the river."

"Thanks, Mister. Mighty kind of ya. I'll return the favor when my head stops spinning." Sam closed his eyes and soon was asleep.

Two days later, Sam woke up alert and clear headed. The trees and the ground were in their right places when he sat up. His mouth watered when he smelled the bacon. He was so famished that he could eat the whole pan of biscuits John was cooking! John handed him a cup of coffee, it tasted so good. "What happened?' Sam asked. John relayed for the third time what happened. "I owe my life to ya, John," Sam said.

"Never mind. Just thank the Lord for saving your life," said John. "Gave me some thinkin' time. I like the peace and quiet here by the river. Take it easy today and we'll head out for Ogallala tomorrow morning."

THIRTY-TWO

A Promise to God

As John and Sam spent a couple of days crossing into Nebraska, they shared stories about their lives. Sam asked lots of questions.

"So, you're a man of faith?"

"Yeah. As a traveling preacher, I stop by isolated homesteads to baptize children, conduct weddin's, bury the dead and listen to people talk about their worries."

"How'd ya get into that line of work?"

"Well, it was one of those life threatenin' situations when I prayed to the Lord that if I survived, I would dedicate my life to Him. So, here I am."

"What happened?" Sam asked.

"Sam, you're askin' me all the questions, but you've told me nothin' about yourself except about leavin' that woman ya loved. What was her name... Patty? No, Peggy. That was it."

Suddenly, Sam wanted Peggy desperately. He was quiet for a few minutes. "You're right, John. I'm a loner like most of the cowboys out here on the prairie. I don't talk much about myself or my history."

"Why not? Ya have secrets? Are ya runnin' from the law?" John demanded.

"Naw, I'll tell ya after you finish your life and death story."

"OK, I'll hold ya to it," John said, then went on. "In the early 70's my brother Mathew and I loaded up our belongings and our families to head west from Ohio. We believed there was free land and opportunity. It took us weeks, but we finally found land that would support our two families. We were near Indian Territory but were close to Fort Supply so we thought we'd have protection from the Indians. We plotted out our land next to each other, built dugouts to live in until we could afford to build a decent house. We tried plantin' a garden for fresh vegetables but they all died. Too hot and dry.

"We'd brought some livestock with us and bought more in Dodge City. The cattle survived and produced some calves. We knew that was the future for us. That first winter was so cold those cows gave icicles. The ground froze so hard there was nothin' for 'em to eat. Mathew and I rode two days in a bitter cold wind to buy some feed from a neighbor. We lost Mathew's wife and daughter and one of my daughters to the fever that winter. Couldn't even give 'em a decent burial with the ground frozen so deep.

"One early spring day, the neighbor who'd sold us the feed rode over to warn us that the Comanche had organized an enormous war party. They were angry about the white buffalo hunters destroyin' their livelihood. They were headed to Adobe Walls and were pickin' off any white settlers and hunters they came across. The neighbor moved on to warn others.

"Me and my brother talked about what to do. I didn't believe we could make it to Adobe Walls before the Indians would catch us. Mathew thought we should make a run for it, but he finally agreed with me. I was right. In a few hours, as we were stackin' up dirt, rocks, pieces of wood, anything to create a barrier in front of the dugout, a party of Comanche galloped across the field toward us. My wife, Louise, our young daughter, Maddie and Mathew's second daughter, Jo Anna, huddled inside against the far wall of the dugout. Mathew, my son Thomas and I took up positions behind the barrier but it was useless against what seemed like over twenty-five warriors. I was hit almost immediately. Then both Mathew and Thomas were shot and killed. They fell on top of me. When the braves came to check, they assumed all three of us were dead.

"During the whole incident, I was prayin' to the Lord and promised Him if I got out alive, I would devote my life to Him. Of course, I was prayin' that my wife and the two girls would survive too. But that was not the plan He had in mind. The two braves who climbed into the dugout killed Jo Anna and my wife who was pregnant. I was losin' blood, goin' in and out of consciousness. Finally, it seemed very still. I managed to crawl out from under Mathew and Thomas, and inched toward the dugout. I saw blood everywhere. I was horrified! My wife and Jo Anna were lyin' on the floor. Maddie was missin'.

"I tore up my wife's dress to bandage my head to stop the bleeding. Then I stumbled outside. It was devastating. The timbers in the shed we had built to house the feed for the cattle were still smoldering but the feed had burned quickly. Even the ground where the prairie grass had been greenin' up was smokin'. The warriors had set fire to anything that would burn including the sod that covered the dugout. I walked around in a daze, the smoke burnin' my eyes and throat. I almost stepped on poor Maddie who lay face down in the dirt a few hundred feet from the dugout. Probably one of the braves wanted to take her back to the tribe to grow up as a slave and either he dropped her as he galloped away or she wiggled out of his hands and fell. Better she was dead than end up an Indian captive. Since everyone was dead except me, I realized that God must have a plan for me that was not homesteadin' the prairie."

Sam rode next to John in silence, his thoughts tumbling. He saw the contrasts between the story that John had shared and his own story of leaving his wife and children to save his own skin. John had lost his whole family in a brutal Indian attack; he, Sam, had abandoned his wife and five children because he was afraid.

Finally, he said, "So sorry. Hard to lose your whole family like that."

"Yeah," John replied. "It took me awhile to figure out what to do, what God wanted me to do. And I missed Louise and the girls..." He took a deep breath. "Some days I was so sad I couldn't get out of bed. But it's been over 10 years and that doesn't happen so much now."

Before Sam could figure out what to say, John exclaimed, "Oh, look, over there across the ravine I see buildings. I should stop there and see how they're getting along. Come on with me."

THIRTY-THREE

Sam Talks About His Life

*J*ohn and Sam rode up to the barn and dismounted.

"Howdy. We were riding by on our way to Ogallala. Thought we'd stop to say hello," John explained to the tall sturdy man and two youth who came out of the barn.

"I'm John, a traveling preacher. And this here is Sam."

"I'm Ben Smith. And these here are my two sons, Jacob and Jeffrey. Welcome. Want to put your horses in the barn?'

"Thanks for your hospitality," Sam said.

Ben showed them around and proudly answered questions about how long they had been there, his crops and his livestock. Sam admired the house that Ben and his sons had built.

"Very nice! How many rooms?" Sam asked. Before Ben could answer, a woman came outside.

"Hello, welcome. I'm Emily. Come in. We're having stew for dinner. Will you stay?"

John and Sam enthusiastically agreed. They enjoyed the large pot of stew, sharing stories and the friendliness of the Smith family. Later, they bedded down in the barn. In the morning, they got an early start.

As they rode, Sam knew John was going to ask him about his life. He realized it would be easy to put off telling the hard stuff if he talked about his growing up years in Indiana first. So when John asked him, he started with his childhood.

"I was raised in Indiana near the Indiana Iron Works," Sam said. "My dad died when I was four and left me and my mom and my older sister Harriet. I was too young to understand why he didn't come back. I know now, it was real hard on my ma taking care of us alone. She kinda withdrew from life. I was an angry and lonely kid. When I was about ten or eleven I went to live with my uncle, a real character... a farmer and a river boat captain who took frequent trips down to New Orleans. He'd tell us stories about New Orleans, pretty wild town. Taught me how to play cards. I got my wanderlust from him. But he was strict, too. When I was twelve, we had a big argument over somethin' and he threatened to throw me out. I'd had enough. Packed my sack and left. Hiked over to some cousins who lived in Illinois and got work as a farm hand. When the war began, I signed up. Mustered out in Tennessee when it was over. Wanted to see the country so I wandered for a few years picking up odd jobs, workin' cattle, moved to being the dough wrangler. Ended up in Texas and had a homestead there."

Sam knew he was skipping over some parts of his life and stretching the truth some, but what he was telling was close to the real story. He continued.

"I went to Fort Worth to get some corn for the hogs. Got involved in a card game with some drunk local who was a Confederate Grayback. He pulled a gun on me. I shot back and blew out his lamp. I needed to get out of town. Since then I've been on the dodge. And here I am on my way to Ogallala."

"But how does Peggy fit in?" John asked. "You told me about Peggy back there where we camped below Castle Rock."

Sam rode silently for several minutes before he finally answered. "When I was headin' out of Dodge City, I ran into Peggy dressed like a boy. Turned out she'd lost her husband the winter before. She offered me a meal. In return, I built the corral and ended up helping with the cattle. She lost her young son shortly after I arrived. I hung around, watched over Margaret Ann, her daughter, while Peggy was grieving. Winter set in. It was colder than a knot at the North Pole. One thing led to another and she invited me into her bed. All along she understood, I wasn't plannin' to stay. She was a pretty little thing, spunky and independent. Together we built her a house a little smaller than the Smith's. Had good times together, but she began makin' noises about me stayin', getting' hitched, havin' kids. I got scared and took off while she was over carin' for a neighbor's pregnant wife."

"Do ya miss her?" John asked.

"Yeah, like hell. I almost went back after the first day but..." Sam put his head down.

"Ya didn't want to be responsible." John offered.

"I guess. I was afraid she'd get pregnant..." His voice

trailed off as he turned away from John. The same feelings he'd felt about his leaving Delia welled up and tightened his throat. He rode on without saying a word. The wind had come up and was blowing tumbleweeds across the prairie.

"Well, seems yer a cowboy who's still twelve years old and hasn't learned to stand up and be a man!" John yelled over the wind.

John's accusation stung Sam like a shot through the chest. He was responsible. After all, he'd left without getting her pregnant, hadn't he? He'd built her house and helped with the cattle. That wasn't bein' irresponsible!

It was afternoon when they approached another farm before words passed between them again. John dropped back to ride next to Sam. "Come on sour puss. Were ya raised on sour milk? I'm sorry. Let's go visit these folks. You'll feel better."

"Yeah, I'm famished. Could use some grub," Sam said, following John on the trail toward the farm house.

Two Days Later...

Sam had been following John's horse paralleling the Western Cattle Trail. He came up beside John to ride next to him.

"You've told me about Peggy," John said. "But who's Delia?"

Sam gulped. "What do ya mean, do you know a Delia?"

John turned in his saddle and looked directly at Sam, "Can't say as I do. But when you were delirious back there at the river, ya begged Delia to forgive ya. I'm guessin' ya know Delia."

Sam felt his throat tighten and all his guilt rise up into his mouth. He swallowed hard and looked away.

"Hey, I'm talkin' to ya," John said. "Ain't it true you know Delia?"

Sam couldn't respond. John rode in silence too. The silence lasted as the sun rose in the sky. Sam finally responded.

"Yeah, I know Delia. Or rather, I used to know a Delia. What do ya want to know?" Sam asked defiantly.

"What do ya want to tell me?"

"Nothin'. Why's it so important to ya?" Sam had already told John too much.

"It's not 'so important' to me. Just curious. Ya promised. I figure since you was askin' forgiveness back there, that this Delia must be pretty important to ya. Right?"

Sam looked straight ahead, clenching his jaw and grinding his teeth. He said nothing.

THIRTY-FOUR

Ogallala

Two more days of riding and they entered Ogallala where John headed off to meet one of the parishioners of the church the town was organizing. Looking forward to sleeping in a bed, Sam stabled his horse and rented a room in the Ogallala House. He washed the grime off his face and neck, found a wrinkled but clean shirt in his saddle bag, and lay back on the bed, musing about John's question.

I've already talked about Peggy. Why not Delia? Is she really dead? I don't want to find out. If she's alive, she'd be so fighting mad she'd hang me out to dry. Wouldn't want to see me. John's right. I'm a miserable excuse for a man, wretched, worthless, irresponsible, on the owl hoot trail with a yellow streak down my back. Neither Delia or Peggy will forgive me. He turned to the wall, curled up in a fetal position and pulled the covers over his head.

Hours later he heard banging on the door and roused himself enough to hear John calling his name.

"Hey, Sam! Sam, are ya there? Get that lazy body outta bed!"

Sam staggered toward the door and flung it open to

John's big grin. "Hey, cowboy, wake up! Let's grab some grub. S'posed to be really good here."

"I'm comin' but I'm gonna need some of that tonsil varnish more than grub." Sam strapped on his holster and gun as he talked. Then, the two of them rattled down the stairs.

Sam paused at the entrance to the dining room. Would there be anyone he knew? The Ogallala House was filled with railroad men bargaining with Montana and Wyoming ranchers. There were dusty, weary cowboys who'd driven cattle in to sell or ship east on the railroad. Sam knew he didn't look much like the dude who had joined the cattle drive as a cook out of Fort Worth three years ago. His hair was longer now. He sported a full beard and his face was weathered by the Kansas sun.

Still, he wanted to be prepared and his eyes darted quickly around the room and was relieved when he realized he didn't recognize any of the men.

"Let's grab that table over there." Sam motioned toward the right of the room and led the way.

After dinner, Sam headed to the saloon, leaving John happily greeting folks in the hotel lobby and inviting them to his morning service.

THIRTY-FIVE

Preaching Redemption

Sam found a place to stand in the back of the excited crowd gathered on a grassy field at the edge of town. The atmosphere was festive. It was a special occasion since homesteaders and town's folk didn't usually have time to socialize. Neighbors greeted each other, families sat together on blankets with baskets of food to share, mothers gathered their children to sit down. John walked through the crowd, shaking hands, flattering the women, teasing children, admiring new babies and thanking people for coming.

Sam caught his breath as he saw a woman chasing after a girl that looked about two. She had Delia's ample build and wore her hair pulled back off her reddish face. The girl was laughing and running away just like his daughter, Jenny. He swallowed down the sadness and wondered how John was going to talk to this group about redemption.

John stepped to the front. The voices stilled until only the call of the crow flying overhead could be heard. A heckler called out, "Hey preacher, ya gonna save us from our sins? There a lot of us sinners in this here town!"

A couple of men shouted back, "Shut up!"

"Only our Lord and Savior Jesus Christ can save us from our sins!" John declared.

Some in the crowd called out, "Amen!"

John paused and looked around the quiet crowd. "Thank you, everyone, for coming this morning." While he introduced himself and his topic for the morning, Sam looked around at the group of around thirty people. Most of the folks looked up at John expectantly, waiting to hear his message; children tried hard to sit still after fierce looks from a mother or father. Around the edge of the crowd, some of the men squatted or stood, ready to make a quick escape if necessary. Sam's stomach was knotted and bubbling from his indulgence the night before. His neck was stiff, too. Maybe he would slip away to go take a nap, but he was curious to hear what John had to say. He'd at least stay for the beginning of the sermon.

John began the Bible reading from his worn Bible. "Let us listen to 1 Corinthians 1:27-31, - 'But God hath chosen the foolish things of the world to confound the wise; and God hath chosen the weak things of the world to confound the things that are mighty. And base things of the world, and things which are despised hath God chosen, yea, and things which are not, to bring to naught things that are: that no flesh should glory in his presence. But of him are ye in Christ Jesus, who of God is made unto us wisdom, and righteousness, and sanctification, and redemption: That according as it is written, He that glorieth, let him glory in the Lord.'"

"Let's begin by talking about what we mean when we use the term redemption or redeem. Redemption is the idea of buying back. We redeem or buy back something we have lost, an article, some land, a child, our freedom...."

Sam's mind wandered. Could he buy back his freedom? Could he be free from the threat of arrest, jail, hanging? He listened to John more closely.

"Most of us are familiar with the story of Moses in the book of Exodus. God told Moses that He heard the cries of the children of Israel who were held in bondage by the Egyptians. Bondage means slavery. God promised that He would rid them of the burdens of their bondage and lead them out of Egypt. We know that He did that. He redeemed His people."

Sam wasn't sure he understood. He saw puzzled faces as he looked around. This stuff was over his head and maybe for most of the others too. He watched as a couple of the men got up to leave.

"The Bible tells us that we have all sinned and that we must be accountable for those sins," John continued. "And who among us has not sinned? No one. Examine your heart. Have you taken someone else's property? Their land, horse or crops? Lusted after someone else's wife? Some of us abandon our wives and children not wanting to take responsibility, some of us not only lust after another woman but give in to our carnal desires and commit adultery."

He felt weak as a wave of guilt rose up inside. He could feel the bile burn in his throat and quickly turned away, fearing that he would vomit. John was preaching to him. What did he say about being accountable? He heard John's voice again.

"Since we are all sinners by nature, the only way we

can be redeemed is by confessing our sins and accepting Jesus as our Savior. We can all be redeemed by believing that our Lord, Jesus Christ gave his body and blood for our sins. Belief in Him sets us free and redeems us from our sins."

Several members of the crowd spoke up. "Amen!" and "Hallelujah!" Then a clear tenor voice began to sing. "Amazing grace, how sweet the sound..." Others joined in. "...That saved a wretch like me! I once was lost, but now I'm found, was blind but now I see."

When the hymn was over, John waited for quiet, and then announced, "You who are called to Jesus Christ to confess your sins, come to the front."

Most of the adults and older children rose to go to the front except for Sam and a few men standing with him at the rear. Sam's stomach was churning. He felt weak. He stumbled into the man standing next to him who grinned. "Too close to home, eh?"

"I gotta get out of here."

Sam stumbled back to the hotel and up the stairs, flung open the door slamming it against the wall. He collapsed onto the bed, falling quickly into a disturbed sleep. He saw Peggy and Margaret Ann, Delia and his six children pointing and shouting accusations at him. In his dream, he tried to run away but he came face to face with the sheriff holding a gun who announced sternly, "You're under arrest for murder."

"I'm not guilty. It was self-defense!" Sam yelled. "Let me go! Self-defense..." Someone was holding him down. "Adultery... Not guilty!"

He heard John's voice. "Sam, wake up. You're dreaming."

THIRTY-SIX

Learning to Pray

The sky was steel gray; the wind was bitter. Sam tried to shield his face with his hat pulled down and his kerchief pulled up over his mouth. He could smell the snow coming. They had been riding for two days. He was still angry and hadn't spoken to John. Sam believed John had used information that he had told him in confidence. He'd exposed and embarrassed Sam in front of the crowd of people.

"I think we better wait out this storm," John called. "We can take shelter over there." He pointed to what looked like an abandoned one-room sod house. They tethered their horses and carried their packs inside. Dropping his to the floor, Sam went outside to look for something to use to build a fire. He grabbed some brush and some cow chips and ducked back inside.

His limbs began to thaw as the fire in the center of the small shelter warmed the frigid air. John was stretched out on his horse blanket on the other side of the fire with his eyes closed and his head resting on his saddle. Sam stared at him.

He looked calm and relaxed. As if he knew he was

being observed, his eyes blinked open. "Well Sam, are ya going to tell me why ya're giving me the cold shoulder?" He rolled over to prop himself up on his elbow to look directly at Sam.

"Anyone would be pretty upset at someone who takes his personal information shared in confidence and preaches about it in public!" Sam declared.

"Aren't ya being a little arrogant? Do ya think ya're the only one who has shared that kind of personal information with me? Actually, there were others in that crowd who've committed the exact same as yours and worse sins. I was preaching to everyone." John lay back down. "Besides, preaching was the only way I could think of to get your attention."

Sam was quiet, John's words from his sermon echoing in his head. "Belief in Him sets us free and redeems us from sin."

Finally, he looked at John and asked, "How do I do it? Confess, I mean. What do I have to believe to get redeemed?"

"Open your heart to the love from God and accept that Jesus Christ died for your sins. Then ask God for forgiveness. I will pray with ya." John rose and kneeled next to Sam.

Sam felt clumsy as he tried to move from sitting to kneeling. "What do I say?"

"I will lead ya. Repeat after me. Our Lord, God have mercy"

Together they prayed. "Our Father, I have committed sins and transgressions against you and against those I love. I am truly sorry for my past sinful life. Please forgive me and help me to not sin again. In Jesus Christ, we pray. Amen."

"That's all I have to do?" Sam asked incredulously.

"No, that is just a first step… to learn to pray. To be forgiven of your sins, ya must believe and have faith in God and in Jesus Christ, His son. That belief includes accepting that Jesus died to save our souls. That is how we can be forgiven for our sins."

"But, what do I have to do?" Sam was puzzled.

"Through God's grace, He has rescued us and offered us redemption. But first, we hear the good news of the Gospel and then we must believe and fully trust in God and in Jesus as His son sent to earth to save us."

Sam was bewildered. John offered, "I tell ya what, ride with me for a few months as I preach and convert the good people of the prairie to believe in God. You will hear readings from the Bible and explanations of Christian salvation and God's forgiveness. You can learn more about Jesus Christ and his sacrifice for our sins. When you're ready ya can pray and ask for your own redemption and forgiveness."

Sam followed John's advice and joined him for the next several months. He listened to his sermons, he learned verses from the Bible and he prayed. Sometimes he prayed alone and sometimes he joined with the folks who came to listen to John. One day, Sam was praying with farmers and their wives and children in Custer County, Nebraska. He asked for forgiveness of his sins, his abandonment of Delia and the children, his deception of Peggy and Margaret Ann and his murder of the man in Fort Worth. When he finished, he felt a sudden warmth fill his heart and expand through his body. He saw a bright light around him even though he had closed his eyes. Tears flowed and he heard a voice telling him to apologize to Delia and to Peggy.

With John's help, he wrote a letter to Peggy and to Delia in case she had escaped the tornado. Although he provided some information about his life since he had left each of them, the most significant part of each letter was his apology with a request for forgiveness. He found a rancher riding south to Dodge City who agreed to carry the letter and find Peggy's homestead. He mailed Delia's to the postmaster in Weatherford, Texas.

THIRTY-SEVEN

That Night He Was Happy

Eight Months Later

Sam settled his head on his pack and pulled up a blanket to keep off the morning dew. The coals from the dying fire glowed orange and yellow in the dark night. A coyote howled in the distance. Stripe moved in a little closer. The sky was a midnight blue blanket sprinkled with the dust of a thousand stars. The crescent moon offered a sliver of bright light. Sam took a deep breath of the fresh Wyoming air filled with the fragrance of sage. The evening was cool; the air was still. Sam thought back over the last several months of traveling and assisting John as he wandered across the Nebraska prairie baptizing babies, marrying young lovers, burying the dead and preaching the Gospel whenever he could get a handful of homesteaders, cowboys, or shopkeepers to come and listen. He'd heard John's message many times and almost knew it by heart now.

He'd asked for forgiveness of his own sins. He realized he'd been childish and cowardly. John had been right that he had ducked out of his responsibilities. He still felt bad that he had treated the women he loved so terribly. When the guilt threatened to overtake him, he prayed for mercy and left his guilt in God's hands. Afterward, he felt relief. Maybe that was what John called redemption. Most importantly, he had found relief in writing to both Delia and Peggy and asking for their forgiveness.

Today, he had filed a land claim for this expanse of land in Eastern Wyoming that grew mostly sagebrush and rocks. He also bought a mineral claim for $100 bucks thinking that if he couldn't raise horses and cattle on the land maybe he'd find gold or silver instead. He was ready to settle down and start over. Maybe he could find a good woman. He would treat her well, better than he had treated Delia and Peggy. He would be responsible.

This night he was happy. He was starting a new life. No one knew him here. He had no past, only present, and future.

THIRTY-EIGHT

Miss Sarah Armstrong

Sam rode into town on Stripe to order the supplies he needed. He had laid out plans for a corral, a shed to shelter the livestock and a coop for chickens. He had dreams of buying cattle and horses to start his herd. He wanted a successful cattle ranch. As he rode down Main Street, he saw heads turn and thought people were probably wondering who he was. He tipped his hat to the ladies and hollered a friendly "howdy" to the men. One of the young boys ran up and offered to tie up Stripe. "Why ain't ya in school?" Sam had asked.

"Cuz it's Saturday" came the reply. Sam had no idea what day it was or even if it was September yet. "That's a good reason. What's your name?"

"Joey. My pa's inside." He motioned toward the general store with the sign painted above the door, "Joe Dodd's General Store"

"Are ya a Dodd?" Sam asked.

"Yes, sir," Joey replied, following Sam through the door.

A big barrel of a man, with a rim of hair around

his bald head, held out his hand. "Welcome to Dodd's Hardware!" he boomed. "Big Joe's the name." His bushy eyebrows stuck out like an overhang. As he peered at Sam his gray eyes twinkled with amusement.

"Ya must be new in town."

"Yep, been here a couple of weeks. Name's Sam Martin. Rode in from Nebraska. Got me a stake out north of town. I need some supplies and I figured this was the place."

"Welcome to Glendo, Sam," Joe boomed. "I can outfit ya with whatever ya need."

Just then the front door opened and a lovely young woman greeted Big Joe with a warm smile that lit up her whole face. Sam stared. She was petite, barely five feet tall, with black hair pulled back from her face and wrapped in a loose bun at the nape of her neck. Above her high cheek bones, her dark brown eyes sparkled, flecked with gold. She looked delicate with smooth clear skin. She was beautiful.

"Sam," Joe said, "this here pretty lady is Miss Armstrong, our school teacher. Miss Armstrong, meet Sam Martin. He's new in town. Came from your home state of Nebraska."

Sam removed his dingy hat, nodded his head toward her and lowered his eyes. "Howdy ma'am." His heart was thudding so loudly he feared she might hear it. He flushed with embarrassment. He was so tongue-tied that he answered her questions in one or two words.

In contrast, she was friendly and kind. Giving him a big smile as she left. "It was a pleasure to meet you, Mr. Martin," she said. "I hope to see you again soon."

After she left, Big Joe laughed at him. "I guess she bewitched ya, didn't she? She does that with all the boys around here."

"What's her first name? Is she spoken for?" Sam asked.

"Her name's Sarah. She's not taken, but she doesn't much welcome courting from the average frontier man or cowboy around here. Now, what can I help ya with?"

Joe was very helpful in offering Sam some posts a customer had returned, which were cheaper than the freshly cut ones. Sam was reluctant to spend all of the pay he had from the cattle drive but he did decide to buy some of the new fencing called barbed wire.

For the next week, Sam worked putting in posts for barbed wire fence, building the corral and an animal shed. Each day his mind drifted, distracted by the memory of the woman he had met in Dodd's Hardware Store. He listed the reasons to forget about her, to force his mind to let loose of this obsession. He was sure she wouldn't give him a minute of her time. Someone else was probably courting her already. Besides, he didn't deserve her. But she haunted him. She appeared in his dreams at night and distracted him from his work. He imagined having a conversation with her. She would ask how he came to Wyoming. She would want to know about his past. A few days later, Sam rode into town. When he heard a lyrical voice float out from the school house window, he stopped to listen.

"I wandered lonely as a cloud
That floats on high o'er vales and hills,
When all at once I saw a crowd,

A host, of golden daffodils;
Beside the lake, beneath the trees,
Fluttering and dancing in the breeze.
Continuous as the stars that shine
And twinkle on the milky way,
They stretched in never-ending line
Along the margin of a bay:
Ten thousand saw I at a glance,
Tossing their heads in sprightly dance."

His mother had recited that poem, but he couldn't remember its name. It was the only poem he could remember her reciting from memory. Initially, he loved listening to her recite, but after his father died, she repeated it over and over and he got tired of hearing it.

He turned to listen again to the lyrical voice.
"For oft, when on my couch I lie
In vacant or in pensive mood,
They flash upon that inward eye
Which is the bliss of solitude;
And then my heart with pleasure fills,
And dances with the daffodils."

Now, he remembered one time, when his mother had started "I wandered lonely as a cloud…" he ran outside and shimmied up the grand oak tree that spread its broad branches to shade the house during the sweltering and humid Indiana summers. He'd crouched on a thick branch half way up the trunk. The leaves rustled in the breeze, cooling his damp sticky skin. His mother yelled up at him to come down for supper. He'd yelled back, "No! I hate you!" He winced at this memory, regretting lashing out at her. He'd refused to do anything she asked. Then sadness enveloped him as he remembered his grief-stricken mother after Pa died. She'd lost all her gaiety and sparkle. She just repeated the poem as she sat rocking in the dark. How insensitive and cold he'd been to her, too.

He'd felt so alone and sad at that time. He felt as if both his Pa and his Ma had abandoned him. She didn't talk much. She never touched him. She didn't help him learn how he should treat a woman. His uncle taught him how to be tough. "Grow up and be a man," Uncle Bill would demand. Sam would often go off by himself to try to figure things out. Most of the time he was alone and lonely.

He yanked himself out of his painful memories as he heard the voice again. "Children, I want you to draw a picture of the images the poem brought to your mind."

In the ensuing days, he frequently stopped to listen when he passed the school. Her voice, melodic and soothing, reached in to heal the loneliness in his heart. During one visit to town, he had seen her walking away from the Dodd store with a serious limp. He wondered about the cause and he wanted to offer her his arm. Her firm straight back conveyed confidence and self-possession despite the limp. Her hair, as black as a crow's wing, glistened in the sun. He imagined unpinning her hair and letting it fall in waves down her back, burying his face in the softness. He wanted to ask her if he could call on her, but what if she rejected him? Was he worthy of her? Was he ready now to settle down with a good woman and treat her well? Could he support her and be responsible for her and a family now?

THIRTY-NINE

The Courtship

After the church service at the Glendo Community Church a few weeks later, he nervously asked Sarah, "May I call on you next Sunday?"

A smile spread across her face and her eyes lit up. "Why don't you come over for tea this afternoon?"

"Why, yes. I'll come at two." He hoped his response was not too eager.

They sat in rocking chairs, enjoying the warmth of the afternoon sun on her front porch.

"Where did you live in Nebraska?" she asked him. "Didn't I hear Joe say you came from Nebraska? I grew up in the Sand Hills, myself." His heart beat faster as she smiled at him.

He was nervous. But her friendly demeanor put him at ease. "I really didn't live anywhere for very long. I was traveling with an itinerant preacher and helping him out. We traveled all over Nebraska. I don't remember the Sand Hills, but I'm sure we were there."

She told him stories of growing up in Thedford and he shared his from the cattle drive. The sun was setting and the coolness of the Wyoming evening brought an end to the afternoon. Sarah surprised Sam when she said, "Let's have tea again next Sunday after church."

They continued to share stories. She seemed intrigued by his experiences on the prairie. She asked him about his little finger. He told her about his service in the Civil War and how the injury on his hand had not healed properly and left his little finger deformed. She told him about her arthritis which gave her a limp and how it seemed to be getting worse.

They met every Sunday after church to visit and have tea. She complimented him, saying, "You're like my father. You're wise from your life experience in the war and on the prairie."

Sam was touched by her compliment but he worried that she only saw him as a fatherly man, a companion. He wanted more than that.

Sam knew he and Sarah were quite a contrast. He was tall and gangly; she was petite and graceful. He was direct and almost crude with his words; she seemed able to find the right words to touch and connect with anyone—a child, a parent or a stranger—from her heart. He knew he had prairie smarts and a pioneer spirit, but she was refined, cultured and well read. While he was often suspicious and stand-offish, she was open-hearted and gracious.

It was her ability to find the right words to touch him and her open-hearted acceptance of him that encouraged him to share the story of his redemption with Pastor John. He told her about meeting him, hitting his head and riding to Ogallala with him

"After hearing him preach about redemption, I realized I needed to confess my sins and ask forgiveness. I was on the run because I killed a man in self-defense. I hid out on a homestead in the middle of Kansas. I was there for a long time, helping with the cattle and building a house. Then, I got scared. Peggy wanted to get married. I up and left without even saying goodbye. John called me on it"

"What do you mean?" Sarah asked.

"Well, John saw how much I missed Peggy and her daughter, Margaret Ann, who I adored, so he confronted me. Accused me of acting like a twelve-year-old. Running away,not being a man, unwilling to take on responsibility for a wife and children. John's sermon convinced me I needed to be saved from my sins. I didn't even know how to pray. So John got down on his knees with me and guided me through it. I couldn't have done it without him."

"He must be a very good man," Sarah said.

"Yeah, I owe him a lot. So I rode with him for a long time helping out and sometimes telling stories. He baptized babies, married couples and preached anytime he could get some folks together. I finally accepted Jesus Christ and asked him to baptize me. Since my baptism and conversion, I am a new man and ready to settle down."

"I'm glad you told me that story. I wondered about your history and why you didn't have any family."

The following week, as Sam reflected on telling Sarah this story, he asked himself why he was willing to confess so much to her. She accepts me, he thought. She makes me feel better about myself. I'm willing to be responsible now. She didn't reject me when she heard about my sinful ways.

Still, it felt too risky to tell her about abandoning Delia and the children. Would Sarah forgive him for that? The guilt rose up inside as it did every time he thought about his family. He was pretty sure now that Delia and the children were dead. He had never heard anything back from the letter he'd written asking her forgiveness.

The next time they met, Sarah asked if he would like to hear some of her favorite poetry. He eagerly agreed, although he was concerned she would find him crude and unrefined. Instead, she laughed and seemed to delight when he remembered lines from a poem she read to him from the week before. Each time, he vowed to tell her about Delia. Each time he didn't. He was sure that if he told her, she would not want to see him anymore. He couldn't bear how lonely he would be.

Instead, he went to church every Sunday to pray for forgiveness. He helped the children in the school with supplies, clothes and winter jackets. He was generous to families who needed help on their farms. He became more friendly and relaxed with the townspeople. He stopped to help the widow lady with her groceries.

He was sure Sarah did not consider him a suitor, but he hoped she knew he admired and respected her. She seemed happy to see him when he came each Sunday afternoon. He had told her how much he liked listening to her reading poetry. He came by to help her navigate the ice and snow walking to school since her arthritis was worse in the winter and her limp quite pronounced.

After a cold snowy winter, Sarah and Sam were enjoying the sunshine, sitting on the porch drinking tea.

The sun had melted the snow, turning the road into mud. Wildflowers poked colorful heads toward the sun.

"Remember a year ago when you asked me over for tea?" Sam asked.

Sarah nodded."I wanted you to feel welcome. You seemed so shy and lonely. You've become a different person. More talkative, friendly and helpful to everyone."

"Because of you. You've welcomed me and, more than that, you've accepted me as I am– a rough cowboy without the formal schoolin' to say things as pretty as you do."

Sarah laughed and began to recite "Give All to Love, by Ralph Waldo Emerson.

"Give all to love;
Obey thy heart;
Friends, Kindred, days,
Estate, good fame,
Plans, credit and the Muse,–
Nothing refuse."

He interrupted her to finish the last stanza.

"Tough thou loved her as thyself,
As a self of purer clay,
Though her parting dims the day,
Stealing grace from all alive,
Heartily know,
When half-gods go,
The gods arrive. "

Then Sam handed her a piece of Wyoming jade that he had found in the Laramie Mountains. "It's rough around the edges like I am but it represents my steadfast love."

Her eyes misted. He plowed on, wanting to say

everything before she rejected him. "Will you be my wife? I know I'm much older, but I promise to cherish and take care of you. I want to spend the rest of my life with you."

Much to Sam's surprise, Sarah responded without hesitation. "Yes, I will be your wife."

PART 3: WIDOW'S BENEFITS

1912

FORTY

The News

The January sky hung close to the ground, spitting a slushy snow, adding a layer of ice to the frozen mud. The wind gusted out of the north with chilling force. The three older boys were staying in town so they could get to school more easily, Charlie with my mother and Daniel and Joe with my brother Robert. I had taken out a land claim about four miles outside of town. It had been a year since Sam died and we had been in Nebraska almost eight months.

"Petey, take Patricia and go do the chores," I said.

Petey wore one of Charlie's old winter coats and a hat from Joe. The coat almost hit the ground and the sleeves hung down to his knees. The hat was held off his face by his ears, but with his face and neck wrapped in one of my knit mufflers, only his wide brown eyes were visible.

"Patricia," I added, "you feed the chickens and help Petey with the other chores."

I had bundled Patricia in so many layers she waddled. She had a clumsy gait as she struggled to keep her feet in the hand-me-down boots which were twice the size of her small feet. I'd wrapped her head and shoulders with one of my shawls, leaving only her blue eyes smiling at me.

My joints ached this morning. If I walked more than a few steps my right knee collapsed with sharp pain.

Daniel had ridden out from town last night. "Ma, Uncle Robert told me that the government man was in town asking directions to our place. I thought you'd want to know."

I sucked in my breath. "Is he coming tomorrow?"

"That's what Uncle Robert heard. Maybe he'll tell you about your Widow's Benefits. For your sake, I hope so. I don't like that you have to live out here in this tent."

Before Daniel left I had asked him, "Will you break the ice in the water barrel and check to be sure there's enough water there to last a couple more days. Will you and Joe come back in a few days to take the barrel to the river and fill it up?"

"Sure, Ma," Daniel reassured me. "Anything else you need?"

"No, I'm just glad you boys have all found some work. Your earnings really help."

Daniel and Joe were helping out on Robert's farm even though Robert lived in town. They rode out to feed the livestock and milk the cows before school. They were both doing some special chores on other farms whenever they could like repairing fences or tracking down lost animals. They turned almost all of their earnings over to me to buy food.

After Daniel left, I said a prayer, hoping for a decision to give me the Widow's Benefits based on Sam's war service. I thought about how things would be different if I could get those benefits. We could make ends meet. I wouldn't have to worry about the chickens not producing in the winter. We could use the older boys' earnings to buy more feed and livestock. We might even be able to buy materials to build a real house. Then we wouldn't need to go through another winter living in a tent. And I could buy all of the children winter coats.

As I waited for the government man to come, I thought about school. I prayed each day that the school board would decide I could teach in the county. School boards frowned on married women teaching school but since I was a widow they might allow me to. My best opportunity would be if another teacher moved or got married and I could take over her class.

I straighten up the beds, cleared the dishes and put some corn cobs on the fire to warm it up for the government man. Then I laid down to rest, hoping to ease my aching joints. When Petey and Patricia came back from feeding the animals giggling about something, I told them, "Children, walk up to the rise where you can see the road. Watch for our guest. As soon as you see him coming, run back to tell me."

I must have dozed off because I was startled as Petey ran into the tent yelling, "Ma, the man's here!" I rose slowly while I waited for each joint in my hips and knees to loosen up. I willed my legs to move to the flap of the tent, grabbed my shawl and stood outside sheltered from the wind by the tent.

I watched a well-dressed gentleman struggle along the road. He was trying to stay on the edge of the path carved in the frozen sandy mud, but it was slippery and the ground was rough. He slipped and stumbled frequently. His gray felt hat was pulled down to his ears and he wore a maroon knit muffler wrapped tightly around his neck, covering the lower part of his face. His hands were jammed into his coat pockets. As he came closer, I could see a determined face set with a neutral expression. He didn't smile but he wasn't frowning either. His eyes were shaded by the bushy overhang of his eyebrows.

A sudden dread moved through me. This man was not bringing good news. I shook it off and smiled at him when he caught sight of me.

"Good morning, sir. I am Mrs. Sarah Martin. Welcome. Come in. You must be chilled to the bone!" He took off his hat and unwrapped his muffler, revealing reddish brown hair and sideburns.

He bowed his head in acknowledgment. "How do you do, Mrs. Martin. Thank you. Yes, I am a bit chilled. The warmth in here feels good. My name is Henry Jones." He raised his eyebrows slightly as he looked at me with intense slate gray eyes. His glance around our tent took in the children standing close to me and our meager furnishings. His look was observant and concerned but his smile conveyed warmth.

"Children, sit over on the bench and study your letters. Mr. Jones, come and sit at the table by the stove to get warm." I took my seat, breathed deeply and clasped my hands to keep them from shaking.

Mr. Jones looked at me with compassion in his eyes but his voice was clipped and abrupt.

"I am from the Bureau of Pensions. I am sorry to have to deliver this news." I swallowed and sucked in my breath.

"You're not Mr. Martin's legal wife so your children are illegitimate. You are not eligible to receive Widow's Benefits."

"What? How can that be? How can that be? You must have the wrong information. I am Mr. Martin's wife. We were married here in Thomas County."

Mr. Jones paused, took a breath and said, "Yes, I know you were married here. But unfortunately, Mr. Martin had another wife before you. He was not divorced when he married you. That marriage was still legal. So you are not his legal wife."

"How can that be?" I repeated as disbelief and shock crashed inside and spilled over into tears and sobs. "I can't believe that's true. How do I know that you have correct information? I am sure what you have is wrong."

"We have documented it well, including interviewing Mr. Martin's first wife. I am sorry to have to tell you that you will not receive any benefits."

"How can we live?" I sobbed.

As he watched me dissolve, he kept murmuring, "I'm sorry. I'm so sorry."

Just as I was about to quiet myself, I remembered the imminent decision from the school board. The force of humiliation and shame of "illegitimate" struck me hard. I couldn't breathe. Sobs racked my body as I struggled for control. "They'll reject me. I won't get the post."

Mr. Jones started to reach out to touch me, then thought better of it. "Now, now," he crooned. "I'm sure you'll manage."

Between sobs, I pleaded with him. "Please, sir, don't tell anyone here. Please don't share this information." I wanted to make sure Mr. Danzier, the school board president didn't hear about this since he was already spreading rumors about me.

Mr. Jones gathered his eyebrows into a frown. He let out a huge sigh, looked at me closely and nodded his head. "I won't reveal this information to anyone in your community. I promise." Then he apologized again, "I'm so sorry to have to tell you this. I will leave you with this letter that explains the official decision and the information we have about the case." He handed me the letter and then awkwardly backed out of the tent carrying his hat and muffler. I couldn't bear to read it now so I put it away in my wooden box with my other important papers. Then I sat down, put my head down on my arms and sobbed until my head throbbed.

My son put his hand gently on my shoulder. "Mama, what is wrong? Why are you crying?" When my sobs quieted, he helped me stand up and led me to the bed telling me, "Mama, you need to rest."

I fell into a deep sleep. It was dark out when I felt him shaking my shoulder. "Mama, I made cornmeal for Patricia but it is night time now and we are hungry."

Now six, he was such a good boy. I felt the swell of love filling my heart. Then a wave of panic and fear rose and closed my throat. What was I going to do? I struggled to get up to fix something for the children to eat. My mind swirled from one question to another. How would I cope with this devastating news? How would we make ends meet? Would I still be able to get a teaching position? What would I tell the boys, my mother, my brothers and sisters, folks in the community?

I went through the motions of making biscuits for the children and frying a little salt pork for them. The lump in my throat was enormous. I couldn't eat.

When I woke up the next day, it was still dark. I was curled in a ball, with my arms wrapped around myself. I was so stiff, I couldn't move. I felt nauseous. I lay there, gradually unfolding my stiff body, taking deep breaths to calm my racing heart. When I finally got out of bed, I relied on habit to fix a breakfast of porridge for the children.

"Petey, Mama's not feeling well. You're such a good reader, will you read to Patricia and help her with her letters?"

FORTY-ONE

Looking for Answers

I sat in my rocking chair with my Bible open on my lap, hoping for inspiration and answers. Instead, I sat there lost in reverie, trying to find answers by going over my life with Sam.

I remembered when I first saw him years ago at Dodd's General Store in Glendo, Wyoming. He was tall, lanky and so handsome. His eyes twinkled and crinkled at the corners when he caught me looking at him. At first, I thought they were brown but, later I discovered they were hazel, sometimes brownish green and other times light blue or gray. I noticed a deep wave in his black hair that fell over his forehead when he leaned down. He had a ready grin even though he seemed tongue-tied when Joe Dodd introduced us. He had the hands of a rancher, rough with dirty nails. I figured he either worked his own land or he hired out to someone in the area.

I remembered seeing him on the street one day and wondered if he was married. My mother's voice pushed into my awareness then, "Sarah, you're way too smart and too fussy for a man to be interested in you." I had decided that mother was right and pushed any ideas of marriage out of my mind.

When Sam began coming over, I enjoyed his company and thought of him as a contemporary of my father. I was so pleased to have someone to share poetry and read stories that initially, I didn't think of him as a suitor. He seemed to need someone to talk with, share his hopes and confess his demons. I thought his closed and suspicious ways came from his sense of abandonment when his father died. I liked being around him and how he treated me. He was a gentleman, polite and helpful, yet not obsequious about my deteriorating health. He was quiet and thoughtful. He was so much more responsible than young suitors who had come around in the past. I was surprised when he blurted out, "Will you marry me?" I couldn't resist. I don't know if I loved him, but I cared for him. Being with him was so comfortable and reassuring. Even then, I knew I might be a widow for a long time given the thirty-year difference in our ages.

It never occurred to me that he had lied when I asked him if he had ever been married. He not only lied to me, but he had also lied to my brother and my whole family! At a big family dinner, Robert had asked, "Sam, ever had a wife?" And before Sam could answer, "And if not, why not?"

Robert posed the question above the din of utensils and dishes, multiple conversations and children hollering at the table. Suddenly, everyone stopped talking, staring at this quiet stranger who seemed so out of place with our rambunctious clan. Sam had gulped and looked at me in desperation. I knew he had an answer. I wasn't concerned. Then he had turned to Robert and asked politely, "Pardon me, sir. What was your question again?"

Robert repeated, "I asked why you've never gotten hitched? You afraid of gettin' tied down?"

I watched Sam's face and wondered how he would answer. I caught a dark shadow in his eyes. I thought he was annoyed that Robert was prying. Sam chuckled, grinned, then his eyes lit up and he responded. "Well, Robert, I've been fightin' in the army, ridin' the prairie for cattle drives, workin' a mine and recently buildin' a fence and a house on my 'stead. I had nothing fit for a woman or a life that could support a family. Now my place is ready and I found the perfect woman to share it and my life." He turned and grinned at me in his adoring way. He had handled it with aplomb and none of us thought about it again

Now as I remembered that evening, I asked myself, "How could he masquerade like that?" I was stunned and angry. I felt betrayed. Not only did he lie and mislead me and my family, he had ruined my life and the life of my children too! How could I tell them that their father was a liar and a bigamist? That they were illegitimate?

"What did the Government man tell you?" Daniel asked when he and Joe rode out to help with the water barrel a few days later.

"Mr. Jones needed more information and asked me some questions about your father's life before I met him. I told him I didn't know." I hoped God would forgive me for lying.

"But Ma, when are they going to tell you?" Joe asked.

"You need the money."

I was too embarrassed to tell the boys the real reasons I wasn't going to get any Widow's Benefits. I changed the subject.

"How are you doing in school this term? Daniel, I hope you are getting good grades in history. And Joe, is your spelling improving?"

"Oh, Ma. Leave me alone. Uncle Howard says I'm doing better." Joe was reassuring me by mentioning my nephew who was his teacher. "I'll go get the water barrel loaded on the wagon to go to the river." With that, he dismissed me and my concerns.

Before he went out to help Joe, Daniel responded to my question. "My grades are good. I really like history. By the way, Ma, we are learning more about the Civil War and how the Southern states have taken away the Negro rights using Jim Crow laws. I think about Alida and George. Good thing they live in Kansas. It was a good place for Negroes to go."

"Hey Daniel, get out here to help," Joe hollered.

"Hold your horses! I'm coming.." Daniel headed out of the tent.

As the days passed, somehow I managed to get the children fed and the chores done. I would ask Petey to play with or read to Patricia. Then, I would collapse into my rocking chair to comb through the memories of my life with Sam. I turned over each memory like a rock in the field looking under it for clues, searching for a word, an action, an emotional response to explain how I had so misjudged Sam's character.

Among the rocks I turned over, was the frequency of our moves– from Wyoming to Nebraska to Oklahoma to New Mexico. I had agreed and understood our first move. Sam wanted to keep his homestead in Wyoming, which he had proved up, and file another claim in Nebraska near my folks. But the second move, I did not like nor understand.

After a few years in Nebraska, he had proposed that we move to Oklahoma where the Indian Territory was going to be available to settle. He argued that we could get a claim as well as buy additional land to increase our holdings. He'd then expand his herd of horses. I didn't want to leave the Nebraska Sand Hills or my family. He promised we would return and I finally agreed to please him. But I was reluctant and disappointed to leave my family. Against my better judgment, we moved again to New Mexico for Sam's health.

He had always been secretive and somewhat moody. It was worse before I agreed to move to Oklahoma. I wanted to know more about what it was like there.

"What will it be like in Oklahoma? Why do you want to move there?" I asked.

"I've already told you. I'm not going to talk about it anymore." He crossed his arms, set his jaw and pressed his lips closed. There would be a tightness around his eyes. He would retreat to the barn rather than supper with us. It was probably best that he frequently took refuge in the barn because I didn't like the dark cloud of anger that swirled around him. Still, it wore me down and I lost my resolve.

When he got his way, and I agreed to move the family to Oklahoma he was happy, whistling, teasing the children, and helping me out with chores in the house. His eyes twinkled and I was reminded again why I had married him. Had he wanted to move because he was afraid his other family would find him? Maybe the move didn't have anything to do with horses and a larger homestead.

During our years in Oklahoma, Sam often left. He always had an explanation that made sense at the time. At first, he was looking at a horse or a pony to buy. Those trips were short and he often brought home the horse. There were no clues under that rock. But as his health deteriorated from his asthma and war injuries, he decided to apply for Veteran's benefits. He explained he had to meet with the government people in person in Oklahoma City. They were asking questions about his service and he needed to fill out papers. He would be gone several days, maybe more than a week. There were more trips after that. He often came home in a bad mood, agitated and discouraged. Did he resent us? Was there a clue under this rock? Maybe he was seeing his other family.

When I was pregnant with Petey, Sam's doctor told him he needed to spend winters in a warmer climate. Another rock to turn over. He would leave for about three months at a time each year, saying he was going to Phoenix where it was warm. But was he really in Phoenix? Was his health the real reason? At the time, I accepted it, begrudgingly but dutifully. Now I was suspicious. He had left me in the Oklahoma winter to take care of livestock, his horses, the children and our place. The boys were a great help and we had good neighbors who stopped by to check on us. My own health was stable then, but it was lonely without him.

I got along, but it was a hardship I endured for the sake of his health. Maybe there was a clue here.

After several days of sitting in my rocking chair, reviewing my life with Sam, I thought about our move to New Mexico. He was almost seventy and his health was much worse. His movements were slow and awkward. He often could not control his coughing and he needed to rest frequently. Finally, he decided to sell his beloved herd of horses and our homestead, which we had proved up. He would buy us all tickets on the railroad and ship our household goods out to New Mexico where clean and fresh air would help his asthma. I argued with him, resisting another move.

But he was insistent. He argued that his health wasn't going to hold out in Oklahoma with the prairie dust blowing in the incessant wind. He said he didn't want to be separated from his family in the winters any longer. He wanted us to be with him in New Mexico. He thought he wouldn't need to go to Phoenix so often. He must have suspected he didn't have long to live.

The railroad flyer he showed me said the air in New Mexico was clear and good for asthma. It would be closer to Phoenix if he did need to go to meet with the government people and his new doctors. He wouldn't have to be gone as long. Of course, I agreed. I didn't want to shorten his life by staying in dust-ridden Oklahoma. Were there clues under this rock? Were there other reasons to move to New Mexico?

He did finally receive his Veteran's Benefits just a few months before he died. Maybe he was telling the truth when he said he was meeting with the government to answer their questions and fill out the forms.

I wondered about the strange words he kept repeating in his delirium just before he died. "I won't answer." And something about being "married to Sarah Armstrong Martin." I wondered then what that was about. But I had put it aside with the challenges of getting ready for our trip home to Nebraska. Maybe he was asked about that other wife?

After reviewing all these memories, I still had no answers but Sam's mumblings were another rock that might hide clues to explain his betrayal.

FORTY-TWO

Teaching School

1915

I got the children up in the dark after I stirred the fire in the stove and put on some kindling. We had porridge with fresh milk then gathered our books and lunch to ride to school. Petey rode his own pony and Patricia rode with me on Sally. Soon Patricia would be old enough to ride by herself, but for now, it was nice to have her ride with me.

My nephew, Joseph, left the gate open for us since my fingers could no longer manage the wire closure. Petey jumped down to close it. I said a prayer for Joseph's older brother Howard who was in the army. Last fall, I had stopped by to visit with my older sister Bernice when Howard, who was teaching school in town, announced that he had signed up for the army.

Bernice stared at him, her mouth open. "You did what?"

"I have enlisted," he said quietly.

Bernice ranted at him, but two weeks later he left

on the train leaving Bernice and John to worry about his future.

I had mixed feelings about his departure. As his aunt, I was worried about him and prayed for him often, but his enlisting gave me the chance I was waiting for. I got the teaching position, despite the efforts of the school board president, Mr. Danzier, who was trying to undermine my candidacy. He had spread rumors that I had left Sam in New Mexico. The rumors were so ridiculous that I couldn't imagine anyone believing them. I was thrilled to be teaching again. Besides, it took my mind off Sam's deceit. I was now assured that we would have some money coming in and I didn't need to depend so much on Joe and Daniel.

We had a one-room house now, which was warm and cozy compared to the tent. The older boys had saved their earnings from helping my brothers and working the harvest for other farmers. They especially liked working for the farmers who had been able to buy gasoline-powered tractors. My, how life was changing.

Under Robert's supervision and with some additional help from some of their cousins, they completed a small house and a barn for the livestock by the end of the summer. They'd used wood left by another family that had moved on. The house had a sod roof and one window facing south. The cook stove we'd brought with us would keep us warm when the nights cooled off. I was proud of their ingenuity and their support and I planned to have all three boys move back in with Petey, Patricia and me.

Daniel and Joe were now nineteen and seventeen years old. At the end of a day of working on the house, they would ride off together. I was glad they were getting along so much better than on the journey from New Mexico. I was looking forward to us all being together as a family, but my brother warned me that Daniel and Joe had other plans.

"They're sneaking off to see those Garrison sisters who live down the road from us," he told me. "I don't think you want them to get tangled up with that family. Their kids are none too smart and the older boys are always getting into trouble."

"Oh, I don't believe there is any harm in what they are doing," I said. "Daniel is still very much the man in the family. He's not planning to get tangled up with anyone. Why, just yesterday he talked to Charlie about how important it was to stay in school. He's always asking me what I need and how he can help."

But Robert insisted that both Daniel and Joe had more than a passing interest in these girls. "I still think you should pay more attention," he said. I assured him that I would talk with Daniel and Joe.

FORTY-THREE

Losing My Sons

A few weeks later Daniel came out to help set some fence poles. Afterwards, we sat at the kitchen table.

"Ma," he said, "I'm leavin' next week to take a job on the railroad."

I was sure I hadn't heard him correctly. "What did you say?"

"I know it's hard for you to accept, but I'm a man now. There's nothing for me here. I want a real job and to earn better wages so I can help support you and the children. Then, when I've saved up enough, I want to marry Maggie."

What? A job? Earn money? My heart fell to the floor. Then I was angry. I stood up. "You can't leave. We're a family. I need you here. I don't need more money."

"But Ma, I'm almost 20. I finished school. Uncle Fred helped me get a job on the Union Pacific for good wages. You need money to buy more livestock and run this place. I asked Maggie Champion to marry me next spring. She said yes." His voice softened as he mentioned Maggie. Then he sat up and with determination said, "It's what I'm going to do."

"But I haven't even met her. You can't marry someone you haven't introduced to your mother." I was incredulous.

"You will. I'll bring her out before I leave next week." Daniel stood and took a step toward me.

"No!" I began to sob. Daniel gently put his arms around me and held me against his chest to comfort me. Standing on my toes, I didn't even reach his chin. I felt the strength in his arms and the muscles across his chest. He was no longer a skinny awkward boy. He was a man and he was leaving me.

Two Weeks Later ...

"No, you've not failed your children!" my mother declared.

I was sitting at her kitchen table, having a cup of tea during my usual weekly visit with her in town. She'd sold the family homestead and moved into town shortly after we arrived from New Mexico. It was too much work and it held too many memories of Papa for her to remain.

"Oh yes, I have," I responded.

"No you haven't" My mother wore her graying hair piled on her head to give the impression of being taller than her four feet ten inches. As usual, some of the strands escaped her top knot and waved in the air as she emphatically shook her head. Her eyes, so dark they were almost black, looked at me with the intensity she'd reserved in the past for disciplining small children.

"Daniel has left for a job on the railroad," I said.

"He didn't even talk to me about it before he made up his mind!"

"Well, talk to your brother, Fred. He got him the job. After all, Daniel is a twenty-year-old man now."

I felt the fury boil up inside of me. "How dare Fred tempt Daniel like that without talking to me first!"

With a note of pride in her voice, my mother said, "Well you know how Fred can talk the fox out of the henhouse."

My mother was right. My parents had moved our family from Iowa because my older brother, Fred, had persuaded Papa to homestead on the Nebraska prairie. Of course, the soil was not as black and fertile as the soil in Iowa, but we'd all learned to love the rolling hills with the prairie grass blowing in the relentless wind. Fred had a way with words and could talk any of us into anything and he was very proud of his work laying tracks across Nebraska for the Union Pacific. He probably painted it as an exciting life. No wonder he'd talked Daniel into taking a railroad job.

"But why didn't he talk to me first?" I rested my head on my arms as the sorrow flooded my heart. My family was falling apart.

"And then there's Joe running off to marry Celia Garrison because she's pregnant!" I wailed. "At least he married her. But she's only fifteen. It's a terrible way to start a family. I have failed my sons!" My voice cracked.

Mama was always there for me when I needed to talk. Despite this, I hadn't told her the real reason I wasn't getting widows' benefits. Instead I'd told here I'd been denied because I didn't have all the required papers to prove Sam's service.

My mother wrapped her arm around my shoulder and spoke softly. "Sarah, my dear, you've done a fine job raising your boys. They're kind, generous, respectful and honest. A mother can't be expected to control her sons' behavior when they reach manhood. Their actions are now their responsibility, not yours. Your other three children still need you. You must give them your attention now."

As she spoke, I thought about how Petey and Patricia were excited about learning and going to school. They both enjoyed other children in the classroom. Petey, at nine, loved reading to the other children. Patricia was the youngest and smallest child at school but with a little encouragement would take the center of attention and act out the parts to the stories that Petey read. I didn't worry about them.

Charlie was doing well, too. He would turn fourteen soon and had shot up with his last growth spurt but hadn't settled into his body yet. He had a quick smile for everyone and teased the smaller children playfully. He promised me he would stay in school until he was at least 16. Still, I worried about him and hoped he would keep his promise. He liked the animals and took responsibility to feed the livestock, milk the cows and carry the water. I expected he would be a farmer one day.

Mother was right. I needed to be sure to give my other three children my attention, stop feeling sorry for myself and get out of my morose mood. My older sons were young men and had to live their own lives. I sat up, determined to accept this latest change.

FORTY-FOUR

The Baby's Comin'

Spring was coming on the prairie but the sun still set early. I sat with Charlie, Petey and Patricia at the kitchen table beside the oil lamp. Supper was over and the children had done their evening chores. I was creating lesson plans; Charlie was doing algebra; Petey was helping Patricia with her numbers. My days were long and I was anxious to go to bed. We had to rise in the dark, fix and eat our breakfast and ride into town for school just as the sun was coming up.

Suddenly, Charlie stood up and went to the door. "Someone's coming," he said. He lifted the second lamp from the post by the door and went outside. I joined him just as my nephew Frederick jumped down off his horse, breathing heavily.

His words came in short staccato bursts. "Aunt Sarah, you have to come. It's Celia. Baby's coming. She's in trouble. Her ma won't come. Joe wants you to help."

I didn't hesitate. My son and my future grandbaby needed me. I couldn't let them down. Charlie brought Sally around from the barn and helped me onto the wooden stool

I used to climb up on the horse. Then he boosted me up onto Sally.

I turned to him. "Thank you, son. Take care of the children for me."

"Don't worry Ma. We'll be fine."

Frederick and I galloped down the road in the dark. The sliver of the moon was just showing over the crest of the hill to the east. Clouds covered most of the stars. It was a very dark night. I put my trust in Sally to avoid the prairie dog holes and big rocks that could trip us up.

My thoughts turned to Celia and Joe. She was so young. She must be terrified. Why wouldn't Celia's mother come? Maybe it was the fight I heard they'd had when she and Joe snuck off to get married. Did she really disown her? I'd only met Celia at our last family gathering so I didn't know her very well. I whispered a prayer, asking God to do what was best.

After his wife Millie died from pneumonia last year, my brother Robert invited Joe and Celia to stay in his big house with him. I knew he wanted the company. Joe was already working for Robert on the farm and Celia began doing the cooking. Since Millie was gone, there were no other women in the house to help with delivering the baby. I hoped Robert remembered to get the water hot and have some towels ready. He should know since he'd fathered four children, though just two had lived to adulthood.

As we approached the house, I could hear the fear and pain in Celia's screams. I was suddenly very warm on this cool evening. Frederick helped me off my horse and I hurried as fast as my stiff legs would take me toward the house. The door opened and Joe rushed to embrace me like he was a little boy again. "Oh, Ma, thanks for coming." As he took my shawl, I noticed his normally well-combed hair was damp and tousled. His face was gray, his lips thin, and beads of sweat dotted his forehead.

Robert was nervously pacing in the kitchen. "The water is hot on the stove," he said. I thanked him as he poured some into the wash basin for me to wash my hands then I hurried to the back bedroom.

Celia was between contractions. I sat next to her and took her clammy hand. She moaned and her chin trembled. Her breath was shallow and her eyes dull as she looked up at me.

"May I check on the baby's position?" I asked.

She nodded almost imperceptibly. The baby was in a breach position. Another contraction came, she squeezed my hand so hard that I thought my fingers would break. I was going to need to help this baby come into the world.

But the baby was not meant to live. After hours of labor, a tiny infant girl finally slipped into my hands. There was no cry. The cord was around her neck. She was blue. She wasn't breathing. There was no heartbeat. I turned to Celia.

She saw the sadness in my eyes and began to sob. "No, no." Joe sat on the bed and gathered her in his arms.

My first grandchild was buried in the cemetery near my father.

FORTY- FIVE

"I Will Not Answer"

I stood holding a hand-written document recording the testimony Sam gave on one of his trips to Phoenix. My love for him bubbled up as I read his words, "I am married to Sarah Armstrong Martin." At least he didn't acknowledge any other wife!

I'd finally gotten the courage to go through an envelope of Sam's papers that I had kept in my wooden box. With the passage of almost four years, I thought I could face what I might find there about his past life. Underneath the papers, was a yellowed envelope, worn at the corners. It held several official government documents. Beneath the notification that he would receive his pension, there were copies of depositions he'd given in the previous years. He gave the years of his service, the names of men in his regiment, where he was born in Indiana, and information about his early years. At the time of this deposition he was 68 and staying in Phoenix for his health. We had been married almost sixteen years by then. He reported that he was married to me and that I and our four children lived in Dewey County, Oklahoma. He listed his earlier residences in Thomas

County, Nebraska and Laramie County, Wyoming. There seemed to be some time missing between his war service and his time in Wyoming. There was no mention of other places he'd lived.

The story he told in the documents about his name surprised me, including his claim that he'd been called several names in his lifetime including Sammy by his uncle. He'd never mentioned that to me. He swore his name was Samuel Joseph Martin, that was how I knew him. But he told an unbelievable story about how another boy named William Joseph Martin had tried to enlist in the same company and how the boy was underage and his parents withdrew him.

He went on with the story, "When I was assigned to this company, the name William J. Martin or William Joseph Martin was called at roll call and I observed that my own name was not called. I began to think that I was not a soldier and therefore spoke to the orderly sergeant about it and he said that he had my name and would fix it, but it was allowed to remain that way and I, thereafter, just answered at roll call to the name William J. Martin and I was mustered out as William J. Martin. I never got any discharge paper from said service. We were disbanded at Springfield or discharged there and paid our own railroad fare home."

Sam was good at making up stories apparently. I didn't know what to believe, but I couldn't read any more. Now my anger at his betrayal simmered and threatened to boil over.

I'd learned from one of the men in town whose father

served in the war, that the younger three children might be eligible for Orphan Benefits. Mama encouraged me to find out. Given my status as an unlawful wife, I doubted it was possible, but I wrote letters to find out what was required. I learned that I first needed to prove Sam was their father. All of the children had been delivered at home. My sister had helped when Charlie was born here in Nebraska before we left, but Petey was born in Oklahoma and Patricia in New Mexico. I began writing to the women who had served as midwives asking them to provide a sworn statement that Sam and I were the rightful parents.

When I put the statements I received in my box for safe-keeping until the government told me when my hearing would be, I decided to read more of Sam's depositions. In a document dated almost a year after his story about his name, he was asked several other questions. I was astonished by his answers.

When he was asked, "Who was your first wife?" he replied, "I do not desire to go into the details of that and refuse to say." When shown a photograph of a woman by the government agent, he denied that he knew her. Then he was asked if he knew Delia Sharp of Fort Worth, Texas and if he had ever married her. He swore he did not know her or her sons. Then he added, "I do not care to discuss the matter. I am the man who performed these services. I will not go into my past history." He was a tough one for the government agent.

I guess they had tracked down his first wife. Apparently, the agent had shown her a picture of Sam when he was young along with a recent one, both of which Sam had given him. The wife recognized the young man as the man she had married, but not the old man in the recent photograph. The agent's report said that she identified his withered finger.

After this, the agent confronted him. "Mr. Martin," he said, "you see by this evidence that the soldier William J. Martin was not known by any name except William J. Martin and that he married Delia Sharp and lived with her many years and then deserted her. You claim to be the soldier and have stated you never married Delia Sharp. Which statement is true and which is not true?"

Sam's response was, "I will not answer." Those are the words he had repeated in his delirium! I was riveted as I read how Sam went on to say, "I do not want to introduce any more evidence in this case." Apparently he had introduced a photo in an earlier deposition because the government agent had challenged Sam again. "If you are Samuel Joseph Martin, how came you with this photograph that has been identified as that of William Joseph Martin?"

Sam responded, acknowledging that it was a photograph of himself. Then he said, "I will not state anything more about it. I refuse to state that I am or am not the man described in these depositions. I have said all I will say with regard to my identity and where I have been or my history. I do not desire to introduce any more testimony." It was a wonder he ever received his pension!

"Sam, you liar! You betrayed me!" I yelled. "You were a fake! You lied to me, to my family and to the government. How could you do this?" I was trembling all over. "And you abandoned your first wife!" I covered my face with my hands and sobbed. When the sobs slowed, I was gritting my teeth. The poison from my hatred for him oozed from my pores. I sat down with my Bible to pray, wondering if I could ever find forgiveness in my heart for Sam's deceit.

FORTY-SIX

Proving the Children are Sam's

The bench was hard. I smoothed and straightened my dress again and tucked in a strand of hair that had fallen out of my bun. Joe reached over and squeezed my hand. He knew I was nervous. The Government Pension Bureau had finally scheduled the hearing about benefits for the children. We were waiting in the hall of the Thomas County Courthouse. The hall was eerily empty. The minutes seemed to drag by. The government man was taking the deposition from Daniel who had come home specifically so he could give his deposition in-person. Joe was next.

Daniel opened the door, grinned and walked over to us. Responding to my questioning expression, he said, "It was easy. He asked me about the birthdates of all of us, when Pa died and where we lived. Joe, he'll probably ask you the same questions to verify my information."

"Did he ask you anything about our marriage?" I was worried that the agent might reveal the information about the legality of my marriage. I still hadn't told anyone. I felt too humiliated.

Daniel laughed. "No Ma. I couldn't swear to that

since I wasn't born yet." He sat down to wait with me. "He also didn't ask me any questions about Pa's life after his war service."

Joe and Daniel had repeatedly asked about the government's decision to deny my application for widows' benefits. For a while, I had hedged with vague answers. Finally, I told them that I wasn't going to get widows' benefits because I couldn't prove that Sam was actually mustered out and officially discharged. Neither I nor the government had the document to prove that so there was the suspicion that maybe he had just walked away. Both Daniel and Joe were angry about it, but I felt this was better than the real reason. I shared with them that because of this it was unlikely that the government would award benefits to the children but I had to try.

Joe was called in for his deposition. I relaxed a little.

I had already given my testimony and passed on the sworn statements from the women who had helped deliver my babies. The agent didn't say anything about my marriage to Sam being illegal. I wanted to prove to the government that Charlie, Petey and Patricia were Sam's children. Since they were under eighteen, if the government would accept that they were his children, I held a slim hope they might be able to receive orphan's benefits.

I was still anxious that others who were to give testimony might find out about the illegitimate status of my marriage. In addition to the older children, the agent had suggested that I ask some other family members and a member of the community to testify. So I had lined up my brother Robert, my sister, Bernice and Mary West. Mary was a young wife when she and her husband Harry had settled in Thedford many years ago. She was a long-time friend of my mother's who'd known all of us growing up. She also had attended my wedding to Sam. I thought she would be very loyal to our family, but I had begun to have second thoughts after what Mama told me yesterday.

"I saw Mary talking with Mr. Danzier last week," she'd said, frowning. "Then, when she came over for tea on Monday, she asked why you had left Sam in New Mexico."

I gasped. "I am shocked that she would believe those rumors. Is she getting senile? What did you say to her?"

Mr. Danzier carried a grudge against our family. It began years ago when Sam and I were first married, and he had falsely accused Sam of stealing some cattle. Then Danzier re-routed water from the stream that ran between his place and my brother Robert's so Robert didn't have enough water for his cattle. Robert had taken him to court and won. When I applied for my first teaching position after I returned from New Mexico, Mr. Danzier began circulating rumors that I was still married and had left my husband in New Mexico. He told people such an immoral woman shouldn't be teaching children in our community. Most people didn't believe it and I thought the rumor had been forgotten after almost two years. Now I was distressed that Mary was influenced by Danzier.

"I was furious and told Mary that she knew better than to believe Mr. Danzier," Mama told me. "I said he was spreading lies. But I am not sure she was convinced."

"Oh, I wish I had asked someone else to testify for me. She must be getting senile."

Mama assured me, "Don't worry about her testimony. If she does repeat any of Danzier's lies, the government knows the truth. Relax. It will all work out."

Just as I was recalling this conversation with my mother, Mary walked into the Courthouse. Her testimony was scheduled after Joe's. I rose to greet her. "Thank you so much, Mary, for taking the time to testify for me. "

Her smile seemed forced. She patted my hand saying, "Don't you worry, my dear. I'll tell him that I was at your wedding, that I know you're the mother of the three oldest children because they were born right here. I don't know about your little ones personally, but your mother and father told me about them from your letters when they were born." I relaxed a little.

Joe came out of the room and Mary was called in. It was too late to make any changes now. I took a deep breath. All I could do was hope.

FORTY-SEVEN

The Drought

1917

*T*he spring and summer had been very hot and dry. Crops were dying and the livestock had to be fed grain since all the grass was dried up and brown. The constant wind whipped up the sand, which settled as a fine gritty layer on everything. I tied cloths torn from flour sacks over the children's faces to protect them.

Joe, Celia, and their new baby boy Alexander rode out to visit one hot, dusty evening. After I rocked the baby, Celia settled in to nurse him while Joe and I talked.

"Ma, I want to go out to Wyoming," Joe said. "There's land available to homestead."

"But it's so dry there even in good years," I said. "Remember that I used to teach in Eastern Wyoming. How could you farm there?"

"Uncle Robert says they have developed a system of irrigation ditches that will allow dry land farming."

I looked at the three of them. Pride filled my chest. Celia looked content as she nursed her baby in my rocking chair. Joe was very affectionate and clearly cared for her. They had scrimped and saved their pennies. Despite their youth, they had done well so far. Of course, it helped that they could stay with Robert where Celia did all the cooking and Joe worked hard on the farm. He not only took care of Robert's place feeding livestock, planting and harvesting, but he also hired out to some of the other farmers in the area. Until this year, that is. This year, when green shoots poked through, they soon withered and turned brown. There was so little moisture that the ground either hardened and cracked or the wind blew the sand and topsoil away.

"Uncle Robert is really encouraging us to venture west. He thinks our only option for the future is to go someplace else. Poor Uncle Robert. He's so discouraged, he just sits on the porch all day. He says he is too old to start over, but he wants us to have a future." I could hear the excitement in Joe's voice.

My eyes filled with tears. With Daniel and Maggie living in Grand Island now, this meant I would lose my second son and my first grandchild. I struggled to keep control. I wanted to support Joe and Celia, but I didn't know if I could bear to let them go.

"Whereabouts will you go in Wyoming? How will you get there?" I was full of questions, but was interrupted when Charlie came in from his chores. He began to talk with Joe and as their discussion progressed, it became clear that it wasn't the first conversation they'd had about Wyoming.

Charlie turned to me. "Ma, I want to go with Joe and Celia. I kept my promise to stay in school. I turn seventeen this summer. With the drought here in Nebraska there's more opportunity where it is irrigated."

"Let me think about it," I said, fighting back tears.

The drought had impacted our farm, too. Daisy, our milk cow grew skinny and her milk dried up. We had to buy grain for the horses and the chickens. The chickens didn't lay many eggs. The year before, we had butchered the hog and enjoyed the meat all winter, but I didn't have enough money in the spring to buy another pig. Patricia and Petey had helped me plant the garden but all the seedlings had died. And the four-mile trek into town each day for school was wearing on me. My feet were getting more gnarled and my joints often ached so much at night that I couldn't sleep. With the days away from school during the summer, I was feeling better since I didn't have to get on a horse every day.

I needed some information before I could respond to Charlie's plea. I rode to town to visit Robert. I trusted what he would tell me. I wanted to know more about the irrigation in Wyoming and what it would mean for Joe and Charlie.

"You should move into town." Robert was sitting on his porch looking off at the brown fields, the wind whipping up dirt whirlwinds. The only green was the tall cottonwood trees by the empty streambed.

"With the boys gone, you can't be living so far out of town," he continued.

What he didn't say was that the drought had destroyed my garden and whatever crops we had tried to plant last spring. And, at forty-seven my life would be easier if I didn't have to rise so early to ride into school.

"You should have the School Superintendent's position, you know," Robert said. I had tried not to think about it. There were so many reasons that the school board wouldn't award the position to me. A young man who was newly married had applied for the position. He was a nephew of Mary West's and probably deserved it more than I did since he would soon have a family to support. I'd finish raising my family in a few years. And I was a crippled woman at that. Of course, there was Mr. Danzier, who was now the head of the school board. He argued with anyone who expressed support for my candidacy.

"I've wanted to know if there is anything, anything at all in Sam's background that you know that gives Danzier a real reason to oppose you?" Robert peered at me as if he could find an answer by looking at me.

My stomach flip-flopped. I said evenly, "Not a thing that I know of. Now, tell me about Wyoming. That's why I came in to see you."

FORTY-EIGHT

The Community Meeting

*E*very seat was taken and many people were sitting on the floor or leaning against the walls. In the front row sat the five members of the school board, including Mr. Danzier and Mary West. I paused at the door and looked at the members of the community, parents, children who had been in my classroom, as well as my large extended family. Even Mama was there. There were just a few faces I didn't recognize.

Robert met me at the door and offered me his arm. "Let me be a gentleman and help you find a chair." He led me to the empty chairs in the front row. Soon Mary's nephew Alfred sat down next to me. Mr. Danzier stood up. His face was pocked and jowly and the way he combed his thinning iron gray hair straight back gave him a high peaked forehead. His small shiny eyes darted around the room, narrowing as he caught sight of Robert, Fred, Mama, Joe and other members of my family.

"Welcome, everyone!" he announced. "Tonight we will hear from two candidates for the Superintendent of Schools for Thomas County. I want to first introduce

Alfred West, nephew of Mary West, who is an excellent and experienced candidate for the Superintendent's position." His smile looked almost sinister.

There was a scattering of applause. Alfred stood. He was a tall, thin young man with a rather gaunt face and light brown hair that fell across his forehead. His eyes flitted nervously around the room, never quite settling on anyone. The paper in his hand rattled as his hand trembled. His mouth opened to speak but there was no sound. He tried again. I smiled up at him to reassure him.

He finally began, reading from the piece of paper. "Thank you for inviting me to speak to you this evening. I don't know many of you so let me tell you a little about myself. I live in Loup County, east of here. I have been teaching for six years and recently took over the superintendent role for both Loup and Garfield Counties." As he continued, his words tumbled out so fast it was hard to understand him. Some ran together and made no sense. I did hear him say that he loved children, coming from a large family, and that he believed in high standards. I wondered if others could understand him. Still, there was a wave of sympathy for him in the room. Several people clapped when he sat down with a large exhale of breath. I reached over and touched his sleeve saying, "Good."

"No!" he snapped and moved his whole body away from me.

Mr. Danzier was introducing me. "...Our own beloved teacher with experience in the classroom. It is a stretch to picture Mrs. Martin having the stamina to serve in a demanding role like the Superintendent, but I am sure she would rise to the occasion, if she is chosen."

I was furious. His sarcasm was obvious. What a way to undermine me! During the loud applause, I took my time to rise, allowing my joints to loosen and my fury to quiet. I turned around to face the audience, smiled at the members of the board and the community, greeting them by name. I smiled at the parents and spoke to the children who had been in my classroom. This helped calm my anxiety and gave me strength to address this large crowd.

"Thank you all for coming out this evening," I began. My voice was strong and all my jitters disappeared as I looked at all the familiar faces smiling back at me. "I am so pleased that you are willing to be involved in the selection of the new superintendent. Many of you have known me since before I was married. For those of you who don't know my background, let me briefly review the highlights. I taught in Wyoming for five years before I married Sam Martin. As you know, after his death in New Mexico, I returned home and have been teaching here for an additional four years. I have also schooled all of my five children at home various times, depending on the weather and the distance from school."

I looked around the room and saw that people were listening closely. But I knew that I wouldn't keep their attention for long. "I am not a surprise package. You all know me and my family. So I am familiar and no longer young, new and exciting like Alfred." Several people smiled or chuckled at my self-deprecating humor.

"I believe in bringing out the best in each child, holding high standards while I help each student to achieve his best. I will do the same for the young teachers by supporting them to do their best and setting high standards for their results. The decision you make for the school superintendent is an important one for your children's future. I know you will do it thoughtfully."

There was applause around the room. Before I sat down, I asked if anyone wanted to ask me any questions. It was quiet. Then Mr. Danzier spoke. "Mrs. Martin, you returned here five years ago without your husband. You have stated that he died. But you have not been able to get the widow's benefits you would qualify for since he was a Civil War veteran. I must conclude that it is because you or he was involved in some scandal that has made you ineligible." I heard a collective intake of breath.

How did he know? I was shocked! My anger boiled up inside Even though I hated that Sam had betrayed me, I couldn't allow Danzier to tarnish my reputation or Sam's.

As I gained my self-control, I smiled. "Mr. Danzier, I am surprised that you would accuse a man who fought loyally in support of our democracy, a man who risked his life for his country and who was a good husband and father, of any scandalous acts. You have no right and no grounds for such an accusation." My anger was just under the surface, but my message was strong, powerful and indignant.

A loud voice called, "Danzier, you're a liar!" Another said, "You just have a grudge." That sounded like my nephew. Lots of hollering and accusations erupted. A woman yelled, "We don't want Missus Martin!" "She's no widow." "Danzier's making up stories!" "He's a lying fool." "Danzier should resign!"

Accusations went back and forth. My nephew was nose to nose with Mr. Danzier's son each of them threatening the other. They were surrounded by supporters egging them on.

I was afraid for my safety in this wild crowd. It was so loud, I didn't even hear Robert at my side. I was trembling as he took my elbow and safely ushered me toward the side door. I heard, "Mrs. Martin's a liar too. We can't trust her." A loud "smack" followed. The fight had started. I was so relieved to be outside

"Are you all right?" Robert asked.

My heart was thumping and my breath shallow. I leaned on his arm. "Better now. Thanks for rescuing me."

"Danzier is evil," Robert growled. "He doesn't belong on the school board."

FORTY-NINE

Leaving for Wyoming

We were all sitting around the table after supper in my little house. A cool breeze coming in the door felt refreshing after the hot afternoon. Petey, now ten, sat on Charlie's knee and Patricia, almost seven, was snuggled up with Joe. Petey voiced my feelings when he whined, "Why do you have to go? I don't want you to leave."

Joe and Charlie had come out to say their last good-byes. Robert was taking Celia, the baby, and their bags to the train station. I had acquiesced and allowed Charlie to go with Joe and Celia. They were taking the train and traveling to Western Wyoming to homestead land that had been recently opened up. It was inhospitable, rocky, arid and barren, with occasional bursts of sage brush. I couldn't imagine it would grow anything from what I'd heard. But, according to Robert, the new irrigation ditches made it possible to grow grain and alfalfa and raise cattle. They decided to go now during the summer to file their claim and still have time to build a small one-room house before winter set in.

The previous night, we'd had a big family gathering

with my brothers and sisters, Mama and all the cousins. It had been a warm and boisterous evening with lots of laughter, singing and stories. I'd held my sadness in tightly. I knew I could not hold my family together any longer.

Today as I looked across the table at Joe, I saw a tall young man whose shoulders had filled out. He caught my eye and his handsome face broke into a big grin. With his hazel eyes sparking with excitement and anticipation, and his dark wavy hair, he looked like his father. My heart was heavy as I thought about both Joe and Charlie leaving and going into new territory where they knew no one. Joe's young wife, Celia had tried to be brave but she broke into tears when I'd hugged her last night. She knew she would be lonely.

"Ma, I think you should move into town and live with Uncle Robert," Joe's voice took on an authoritative tone. "We're all going to be gone and you shouldn't be livin' out here. Besides, Uncle Robert needs someone to cook for him now that Celia and I are leavin'."

"I agree," Charlie added. He was entering manhood, stocky, but still a little plump around the middle. Despite my efforts, there was no keeping him here. He had Sam's wanderlust.

I wanted to change the direction of this conversation. "Charlie," I said, "you haven't told me about your hopes in Wyoming. What are you planning?"

"I'm going to get me some land and a few head of cattle when I've saved up enough. I'll be staying with Joe and Celia to begin with. I'll work hard and soon have my own place. Isn't that right Joe?" Charlie looked to Joe for confirmation and approval. Joe smiled and nodded his head.

"Can I go too?" Petey pleaded with Joe.

"No, buddy, you need to stay in school."

Petey's face fell and his lower lip began to quiver.

"You need to stay and be the man in the family since Charlie and I are leaving," Joe added, "You need to take care of Ma and Patricia. Can I count on you for that?"

Petey brightened up and silently nodded as if he understood.

Joe turned to me. "Ma, I want you to move into town and stay with Robert. You would be a big help to him." I knew he was trying to talk me into it by suggesting that I could help Robert. Of course, living with Robert would also be more convenient for me to get to school and I would have adult company.

"And Uncle Robert might be getting electric lights soon," Charlie added, clearly impressed with that possibility. I had also heard there was a project to electrify the small towns and Robert was speaking for it.

"Besides" Joe continued, "in Uncle Robert's big house there's room for Petey and Patricia to each have a bedroom and it would be good for them to be in town. Grandma would like having you closer, too."

"What do you think I should do with my house and the land here if I move into town?"

"You can rent the house and someone else will be happy to farm this land. You can't do it yourself, and with all of us gone, I don't see another option."

His voice rose, as if by getting louder he could talk me into it. Sadness poured through me again as I thought about all of my older boys gone. It would not be as lonely if I moved into town. Robert would be good company and I could see Mama more often.

"Besides," he continued, grinning confidently, "when you become the superintendent you'll need to be in town."

My stomach tightened. I was glad that Joe had stayed out of the ruckus at the community meeting. He had pulled Fredrick off of Danzier's son who was getting beaten to a pulp. That had been about a month ago and the school board had not made their final decision. They had been busy dealing with the petition from the group who had organized to remove Danzier from the board. Still, I was convinced they weren't going to choose me.

But, it was useless to argue with Joe. So I said, "I'll think about it. And I'll talk to Uncle Robert. Now, promise me, each of you, that you'll write at least twice a month."

Joe and Charlie both agreed and then hugged each of us goodbye.

Patricia began to howl and tears ran down Petey's face. I took a deep breath to keep my sadness in check until after they left. I'd continue to see Daniel regularly when he came through town on the train every couple of months, but I knew I wouldn't see Joe and Charlie for a long time. After they rode off, I gathered Petey and Patricia on my lap, held them tight, and let my tears flow.

FIFTY

❧

The Fall

I closed my eyes, trying to close out the sharp pain in my left side and my aching head. The ground was hard. I could feel pebbles pushing into my skin but I couldn't move. Patricia brought a quilt and tucked it around me. Then she ran on her short legs into the house and came back with a shawl, which she folded as best she could and pushed it under my head.

"Mama, don't cry. I'll take care of you. Petey'll be back soon."

Later, in the fog of darkness, I heard a voice I didn't recognize, "We need to move her carefully. She may have broken bones."

I felt myself being lifted gently. Pain coursed through my body. The darkness descended again.

The next time I came out of the fog, I heard Mama's voice. "Sarah, take a sip of water." After a few sips, I looked around. The room seemed familiar. I saw Patricia and Petey watching me from across the room.

"Where am I?"

"You're in Robert's extra bedroom," Mama responded.

"They brought you here after you fell. The doctor doesn't think you broke anything, but you're badly bruised and may have sprained your knee or torn something inside. We also think you hit your head very hard. You've been unconscious for the last several hours. You won't be going anywhere for a while so we thought this was the best place where several of us could take turns nursing you back to health."

Patricia came over to hold my hand. "Does it hurt Mama?"

I started to nod my head when a sharp pain coursed up my neck and to the back of my head. Darkness descended again.

The days merged into one another but one evening, when I was feeling stronger and cheerful, I noticed the breeze had cooled. Autumn was coming on. I loved the colors of the fall. It was the beginning of a new school year. I found the fall combination of sunny days and cool crisp evenings so refreshing.

Robert came into my room to visit. "You're beginning to look more like your old self. Not so ugly. The puffiness is down. The ugly purple bruise on your forehead is turning yellow. Soon you'll be beautiful again."

"Oh, Robert, you don't need to flatter me." I was feeling more optimistic that I would recover. "But I guess this accident ensures that Mr. Danzier will get his way and Alfred will become school superintendent." I felt relieved. The responsibility now seemed overwhelming.

Robert let out a loud guffaw. "Oh, no, you won't get off that easy. The school board asked Danzier to abstain from the vote because of his behavior. Then, the night they were to vote they got word that Alfred was withdrawing. Seems his wife didn't want to live here. She thought the town was too small. She really wanted move to Lincoln or Omaha where she could have electric lights and a telephone. Alfred received an offer from Lincoln and accepted it right away. So the board unanimously elected you as the Superintendent of Schools in Thomas County, with Danzier abstaining. No one believed those rumors that Danzier was trying to spread anyway."

"Oh, Robert," My heart sank. "I know the extra salary would be so helpful, but how will I ever be able to do it?"

"You're getting better every day and soon you'll be up and around. You can tend to things from here until you can get over to the school. Mother and I and Bernice will be here to help you with Petey and Patricia and fix your meals. You concentrate on getting stronger and on what you need to do for school. Here are some papers they sent over for you to go through."

He was too jovial and cheery. I had no energy to look at the papers he'd brought.

FIFTY-ONE

A Challenging School Year

"What are you doing to do about Miss Carlson?"

"She doesn't know how to teach."

"She's mean and doesn't care!"

"She has big city airs!"

"She's too high and mighty."

Several parents sat in front of me, angry and upset at one of the teachers I had hired. She came from a school in Chicago and it was true that she was more sophisticated than most of the parents in Thedford. But that wasn't reason to fire her.

Mr. McCall, who was a crony of Mr. Danzier, threatened, "If you don't fire her, we will see to it that you're fired."

"Wait a minute, Mr. McCall," I said, then looked at each of the parents. "Thank you for coming to me with your concerns. I am very willing to look into the problem. But, don't you all agree that Miss Carlson needs an opportunity to defend herself? After all, we live in a democracy. When people are accused of a crime and come before a judge, they have that opportunity. I need to hear from

Miss Carlson."

Mr. McCall started to object, but the others told him to be quiet and listen.

I continued. "I'll meet with her and discuss your dissatisfaction. I want to hear her side of the story. We'll put together a plan that we all can agree on. I will report back to you by next Monday. Is that acceptable?"

One of the women turned to Mr. McCall, "I told you she'd listen to us. You didn't have to threaten her."

McCall was clearly the ring leader, probably influenced by Danzier. The others seemed more moderate.

Miss Carlson was the first teacher I had hired. She had almost fifteen years of experience teaching young children in the Chicago schools, but she wanted to get out of the city and thought a small rural community would be a good place for her. She was direct and often abrupt with parents, but she was wonderful with the children as long as they followed her rules. Sometimes the rules seemed arbitrary. I could see why the parents might be concerned, although I believed she was a good teacher, just strict. I also thought she was uncomfortable with the parents and didn't know how to talk to them in words they could understand.

After the meeting with the parents, I talked with my sister, Bernice and my brother Robert

"You're right," Robert said, "McCall is one of Danzier's cronies. He's dumb as dirt and can't think for himself. Danzier, on the other hand, is smart, sly like a fox. But I don't think either of them can influence the school board to fire you."

"But it sounds like the parents have a reasonable

grievance that you should look into," Bernice said.

I knew Bernice would have the parents' interest at heart while Robert always gave me good counsel. I was enjoying sharing his home in town and it was good for the children, too. My arthritis was much better since I did not have to get on a horse every day. I also enjoyed the adult company and our evening conversations, especially Robert's perspectives when I had issues at school.

When I asked Miss Carlson to come into my office she seemed frightened and I surmised that she had heard about the parent dissatisfaction. I gently questioned her and pointed out some of the issues. She admitted that she probably didn't need to be as strict with the children here as she was in Chicago. She also confessed that she didn't know how to talk with these parents and really hoped they would just go away.

We were going to meet in two days to put together a plan to report back to the parents, but McCall led several families to raise a rallying cry in town to get rid of her. Perhaps it was a way to tarnish me. The day we were to meet, Miss Carlson came into my office in tears.

"I don't want to be the cause of such a fuss in the community," she said. Then she handed me her resignation.

"But Miss Carlson, I am not asking you to resign. We can work this out. We need a good teacher like you here in Thedford."

Unfortunately, I couldn't talk her out of it. I was very sad to see her go and I had to scurry around to find someone to take her classes.

That was only the beginning. At mid-year, the most

well-liked high school teacher who was in his early twenties started courting one of his students. I called him into my office.

"Frank, you know it looks bad to court one of your own students."

"She's old enough," he protested. She's sixteen. Her parents like me."

"Frank, no matter what you do, it will look like favoritism to the other students. I will move her out of your class and I am asking you to stop seeing her until summer break."

He mumbled, shook his head no and then stared for a long time at the wall. Finally, he said, "All right, I agree."

Unfortunately, I soon heard that he was seeing her again. One of the teachers who was what I called "prim and proper" caught them behind the school in an "embarrassing" situation. The town gossip was fierce.

I called Frank in again and he admitted it. "Mrs. Martin, I can't stop seeing Johanna. We are going to get married."

I found myself awake at night worrying. I talked this problem over with Robert too. He was adamant that I should fire the teacher, arguing that Frank hadn't kept his word and he was a poor role model for the students. But Frank was so good in the classroom and so well liked, I hated to lose him. I kept hoping he would come to his senses, but ultimately, I had to ask him to leave too, with only two months of school left. I couldn't get anyone else to take his classes at that point, so I ended up teaching them myself. It was exhausting to be back in the classroom and continue my superintendent duties too.

In the middle of the town uproar over Frank, Robert had handed me an envelope from the U.S. Government. I went to my room so I could read the letter alone. "We regret to inform you that we have determined your children are not eligible for orphan's benefits due to your illegal union with Mr. Samuel Martin."

Anger toward Sam flared up inside me once again. I could feel my simmering hatred of him flow into every crack and crevice of my body. I stood rigid as this corrosive emotion rubbed me raw inside. Then I heard the back door slam and Petey holler, "Ma, when's dinner?"

Breathing deeply, I hid the letter deep in my wooden box, composed myself, and went to the kitchen to fix our supper. I pushed away my thoughts as I stirred up the biscuits, popped them in the oven and then warmed up the leftover cornmeal. Robert came out and asked, "So what's the report?"

"Negative, 'cause I can't prove he served in the Civil War."

Robert asked some more questions, but he dropped it when I told him, "I don't want to talk about it."

School was in session another few weeks. We made it through without any more crises. The day after school was out, Robert and I sat on the porch enjoying the lengthening daylight and the last rays of the sun. Petey and Patricia were finishing their evening chores.

"Why don't you go out to Oregon to visit Annie?" Robert suggested. Annie was our youngest sister who had moved out there with her husband ten years ago.

"I would love to see her," I said. "I haven't seen her since before I went to Oklahoma over fifteen years ago. She was still a young girl then."

"Then you definitely should go," Robert declared.

I hesitated. "I'll need to check my savings. I don't know if I can afford the ticket."

"You can if I buy it," Robert offered. I jumped up and gave him a hug to thank him.

He was still sputtering when I went inside to write to Joe and Charlie.

FIFTY-TWO

Going to Oregon

Summer 1918

I looked out the window as the train chugged up the mountain. The pine trees stood tall and straight, showing off their greenery against the granite boulders left so long ago by the glaciers' slow move across this land. I was headed to Oregon to visit Annie. Joe had responded to my letter and offered to take Petey and Patricia for the summer. Petey could help out on their new homestead and Patricia could watch Joe and Celia's son, Alexander and their new healthy baby girl, Nellie.

I was settled in the window seat so I could watch the scenery. All the seats around me were empty. I took the time to reflect on my first year as superintendent. I'd settled comfortably into my life living in town. I liked my new position and I loved the school community of parents and children. This was the perfect job for me, being responsible for the education of the children in the entire county. I'd thought I would miss the classroom, but I didn't. Of course, I had the opportunity to go back to the classroom when Frank left. Yes, I liked both being a teacher and superintendent.

I did have some challenges this year. But I realized that I was stronger and better prepared now to face the likes of Mr. McCall and Mr. Danzier. I believed I was capable of being successful. I felt confident making decisions, hiring and even asking teachers to leave. Yes, it was a good year for my own learning.

I was appreciative of Joe for encouraging me to move into town. Living with Robert had been a pleasure. I'd not been lonely and living with him helped me accept that my older children are grown and independent. But Petey and Patricia still needed me for a few more years. I felt the sadness rise as I imagined that they too would move away. But I would learn to accept that as I had with the older boys.

The train rocked back and forth and lulled me into more reverie. I was reminded of the train trip from Oklahoma to New Mexico with Sam and the four boys. Oh my, that was over eight years ago when I was only forty. Thinking of my life with Sam brought up the anger that continued to simmer. I couldn't help but hate him for betraying my trust.

For the first time, I began to explore the possible reasons for his lies. He must have been very unhappy to abandon his first wife. Maybe he was in trouble. He had said he was on the run. Maybe he had committed a crime. There were lots of possibilities. He was probably afraid. Afraid that I would not accept him if he told me the truth. Would I? Could I have forgiven him for whatever he did? His betrayal was very painful but I wondered if I could forgive him now.

I remembered his pleasure listening to me read poetry and his attentiveness when we courted. I thought about his love and responsibility in guiding his children. I was grateful for his sensitivity and support for me as my illness progressed and I became more crippled. I felt his frustration when he could not resolve his request for veteran's benefits. Other comforting scenes and reassuring images from our life together floated by. I remembered his delirium when he was sick before he died.

As my reverie continued, I felt him sitting in the empty seat across from me, humble and contrite. He looked hopeful, waiting for my forgiveness. My cheeks were wet with tears. I looked into his pleading eyes. I paused. Then I whispered, "I forgive you."

He bowed his head and vanished.

At once, I felt lighter. My anger melted away. Somehow, it no longer mattered why he had lied or what happened before we met. He had his reasons. I forgave him.

"Let's contend no more, Love,
Strive nor weep:
All be as before, Love,
   –Only sleep!"

Thank you for reading my book!

Dear Reader,

I hope you enjoyed reading *Sarah's Secret: A Western Tale of Betrayal and Forgiveness.* I certainly enjoyed writing my first fiction, inspired by the lives of my grandparents. It was a special pleasure to know I was channeling my grandmother who was such an inspiration to me. And no, the character of Sarah is not my grandmother but I hope she would like Sarah and enjoy the book. Since I did not know my grandfather nor did I get any personal information from anyone in my family, Sam is totally a fictional character. Imagining his life and what may have happened to him before he met my grandmother was an exciting and creative adventure.

I would love to hear your feedback...what you liked, what you loved and what you hated. Write to me at **bev@bevscott.com**, visit me on my website at **www.bevscott.com** or connect on social media.

Finally, I'd like to ask a favor. Would you write a review of *Sarah's Secret* if you loved it, hated it or something in between? It is challenging to get reviews in today's publishing world. I would appreciate it if you would write a few comments about *Sarah's Secret* wherever you purchased this book.

Thank you for reading my first book of fiction.

–Bev Scott

https://www.facebook.com/bevscottwriter
https://www.linkedin.com/in/bevscott
https://www.pinterest.com/bevscottsf/

ABOUT THE AUTHOR

Bev Scott specialized in serving leaders and organizations as a leadership coach and organizational consultant for over thirty-five years. She taught organization psychology and founded The 3rd Act, a program whose mission supports positive aging. As she moved into her own third act, she started a genealogical journey to learn more about her grandparents and a rumored family secret. She concluded that the story needed to be told as fiction using the known facts as her framework. *Sarah's Secret: A Western Tale of Betrayal and Forgiveness* is Bev's debut novel, the culmination of her long-held desire to learn more about her paternal grandparents, and confirm the whispered story about her grandfather.

Bev previously focused on publishing non-fiction work. The second edition of *Consulting on the Inside,* which she co-authored with Kim Barnes was published in 2011. She has written numerous professional articles and contributed to *70 Things to Do When You Turn 70* edited by Ronnie Sellers and Mark Chimsky. Bev blogs on several sites, including her own, *The Writing Life* on www.bevscott.com

Bev enjoys traveling, visiting with friends and spending time with her grandsons. She lives with her spouse in San Francisco.

What Others Have Said:

Using the plain spoken language of the women and men who scratched out life on the hard scrabble plains in the early days of this young country Bev Scott crafts a sharp picture of the violence and the love that shaped the middle of this nation. Every river crossing, each spring planting reveals the conflicts inside the characters and their struggle to survive in contested territories.

– Jewell Gomez, Author, *The Gilda Stories*

We all grow up with family stories, or pieces of them, though our forebears are perhaps not as adventurous characters as Bev Scott's pioneer grandparents. Her research has uncovered long-hidden secrets, vividly restoring their shadowy lives to the forefront in this historical novel. Reimagining people, revisiting times and recreating places long gone, Scott evocatively invites us to join them on their journey of hardship and achievement, as men, women and children traverse the central plains in the late 19th and early 20th century to establish lives in an often-inhospitable environment.

–Jim Van Buskirk, former Program Manager, San Francisco Public Library, co-author, *Gay by the Bay: A History of Queer Culture in the San Francisco Bay Area*

Bev Scott builds on her own family's story to spin a Western yarn of survival in the face of abandonment and betrayal. The heroes here are not the gun-toting cowboys of the range, but the women and children. They survive and persevere against all odds not because of the man in their lives but despite him and his shortcomings. Every sentence here is vital to the story and moves it briskly through to its conclusion.

– Matt Minahan, former President, Board of Trustees,
The Organization Development Network

Historical Fiction requires the best talents of a novelist and of a researcher. Bev Scott possesses the skills of both. I had the opportunity to read an advance copy of her forthcoming book, *Sarah's Secret: A Western Tale of Betrayal and Forgiveness*. Set in the late 19th and early 20th centuries, the reality of frontier life is brilliantly captured in a work that is based on Bev's own family history. And it is a 'page-turner'. She has done an excellent job and, hopefully, her first foray into this genre is a precursor to future volumes.

– David Stringer, author AMERICA'S LOCAL SERVICE
AIRLINES, History Editor, Airways Magazine

Book Club Discussion Questions

If you are in a Book Club, I would be honored to have my book read and discussed by your club. Here are some questions to get you started.

If you would like me to visit as a guest either in person or virtually, please contact me at the address below. Thank you.

1. How does Sarah's story impact you?

2. Do you feel a strong female character from the early 20th century has a message for women today? If so, what do you feel the message is? What is your definition of a feminist? Does Sarah fit that definition? Why or why not?

3. The narrator changes perspectives in Part 2. What does that tell you about the story?

4. How do you feel toward Sam? Would you be able to forgive him? Why or why not?

5. If you were Sam what if anything would you have done differently?

6. Do you think Sam was truly redeemed? Why or why not?

7. The sub-title of the story says that this is a tale of betrayal and forgiveness. Do you think it is more about betrayal or forgiveness? Why?

Contact me at **bev@bevscott.com**

CPSIA information can be obtained
at www.ICGtesting.com
Printed in the USA
FSOW03n0158080717
35868FS